2ND HUMOROUS BEAT

ACTUAL FUNNY POLICE STORIES

OFFICER
BOB MORRISSEY

Outskirts Press, Inc.
Denver, Colorado

2nd. Humorous Beat Actual Funny Police Stories
All Rights Reserved
Copyright © 2007 Officer Bob Morrissey
V2.0

Outskirts Press
http://www.outskirtspress.com

ISBN-10: 1-4327-0186-X
ISBN-13: 978-1-4327-0186-4

Outskirts Press and the "OP" logo are trademarks belonging to Outskirts Press, Inc.

Printed in the United States of America

To all law abiding Americans who are constantly working for the good of the nation. People who support their law enforcement agencies. They who give and not take. I hope my book will make you laugh and relieve some stress in these trying times.

ACKNOWLEDGEMENTS

Thanks to all the oddball characters that I met while being a
police officer for thirty-three years. This book would not of
been possible without you.

Special Thanks to my wife Mary Morrissey for all She did in
helping with this book. Especially the art illustration.

TABLE OF CONTENTS

PREFACE

Police work has immense responsibility.

A rookie officer on his first day on the job may be put into a situation where in a split second he has to draw his gun and administer the death penalty. If he makes the wrong decisions in that split second it may cost his life.

CHAPTER 1
UNORTHODOX

I was enjoying my ten year class reunion, talking of the past and all the funny things that happened while we were in school. My attention quickly came back to the present when I felt a large hand grab my shoulder. I turned and there stood big Harry Bruno, all six foot four of him. We played football together and he was the toughest, and meanest player on the team.

"Bob, great seeing you again. You're a cop, I got a problem." Right away I wondered who he beat up. "You know I got an exterminator business." I nodded. "Well, every day people come into my place with jars and cans with cockroaches in them. I'm in the business of killing the damn things, not buying them."

I looked at him. "So how does that affect me?"

"I want to ask if you know a policeman who has long blond hair?" I mean long hair down almost to his knees. It seems he tells people that I buy cockroaches for two hundred and fifty dollars a roach. When I tell them I'm not buying cockroaches they get mad and release them in my store. How does it look when a new customer comes in and sees roaches running all over the place?"

I stared at him and thought, what the hell has he been drinking? "I'm going to tell you Harry, there is no police officer with hair all the way down to his knees. Some guys from the Vice Squad wear their hair long but not down to their knees."

"Well, I want to tell you, Bob, if I find out who he is, I'll break his damn neck."

I just wrote it off thinking that some of the hits he took to his head when he played football were catching up to him.

I went back to work. One day I was assigned to work with an officer David Maher. I had never worked with the man before and knew nothing about him. Other officers said he was different. Although he went through the police academy like the rest of us and was taught how to handle all types of situations, he didn't do it by the book. He did it his way. That was the rumor.

Dave was a little older than I and seemed like an intelligent man. He didn't act any different than anyone else I worked with until we got our first call. It was a family disturbance in the toughest part of Toledo. We pulled up in front of the house and I got out of the scout car. I could hear loud shouting, cussing and furniture being thrown around. I was waiting for Dave to get out of the car.

He yelled, "Just a minute, I'll be right there." I kept staring at the house where all the noise was coming from. I turned back to the scout car when I heard the door slam. I could not believe my eyes. Dave had on a thick blond wig. It draped down to his thighs. His eyes were covered with orange framed sunglasses. He pushed his hat down on his head, pointed to the house and said, "Let's go Cat, let's bring down the heat in that pad."

I just stood there and gawked at him as he passed me. I never saw anything stranger in my life. The blue uniform, long blond hair and orange sunglasses looked weird. I followed him up the walk. He didn't go on the front porch, instead he walked around the side of the house. When we passed a window everything went quiet inside. I assumed the people were watching us. A voice from inside blurted out, "Man, there's a jive ass hippie cop coming around the back of the house."

Dave knocked on the back door. A woman answered and I could see the strange look on her face when she saw him. He gave her a friendly smile. "Who's raising sand here?" He formed a peace sign with his fingers. "We bring peace. Lay it on us, what's happening?"

The woman shook her head. "You don't needs talking that down home shit. I's gots' an education." She made a gesture with her hand and we followed her into the front room where about ten mean looking people were glaring at each other.

Dave got their attention when he swished his long hair back and forth. He started to say something but stopped abruptly. He pointed to a large cockroach that ran out of a crack in the wall and raced toward the ceiling. "Damn, look at that beautiful creature. It's an amber finch. Its got to be worth at least two hundred and fifty dollars. They are almost impossible to catch."

Everyone in the room scrambled to the kitchen grabbing bottles, cans, and other containers. When they returned, I shouted, "Who called the police? What was the fight about?"

They forgot what they were mad about. They were staring at the ceiling where the roach was. One of them holding a glass asked, "Who buys these amber roaches or whatever they're called?"

The hair on the back of my neck raised when Dave shouted, "Take them to Bruno's exterminators on Monroe Street. Just be gentle, don't injure the fine expensive specimen. Bruno will only buy them if they're in good condition."

The disturbance was over. Everyone was still holding their containers staring at the ceiling when we left.

Back in the car, Dave took off the wig and sunglasses. He once again was a professional police officer. I told him he did a nice job settling that disturbance, then gave him some good advice. "Better get a new exterminator."

CHAPTER 2
SHOOTING CHARLIE

Some police officers go through their careers never pulling their guns from their holsters. Then, there are others like Charlie. He was always at the wrong place at the right time. The first time I met Charlie he was working Unit 11. I was working Unit 12. Both units received a call from the dispatcher, "Door and Heston, the Night Time Carry Out a robbery in progress." Unit 11 was the first car to arrive and we pulled up behind them. Charlie jumped from the car and ran to the front door of the carry out. The door flew open and the robber came out with a gun in his hand. He fired at Charlie who was six feet away. Charlie immediately returned fire. Both the robber and Charlie emptied their guns at each other. Neither man was hit. Charlie's partner fired one shot and dropped the robber.

It was never determined how both men missed each other at such close range. We figured they pulled the gun down when they squeezed the trigger. This caused the projectiles to go to the sidewalk.

In another incident, Charlie was working with his older partner. The call came in about a demented man with a gun hiding in a parked car. My partner and I walked up on the passenger side of the car and saw a man lying on the back seat. Charlie and his partner approached the driver's side. Charlie saw the guy rise with a gun in his hand. As usual Charlie didn't hesitate. He emptied his gun at the guy. He then grabbed his partner's gun and emptied his too. Glass was flying in every direction. My partner and I dove to the ground.

The guy wasn't hit but seeing and hearing bullets coming at him, tossed his gun through a blown out window and screamed, "I had enough of this shit. Quit shooting."

One night an angry mob surrounded Charlie. They were pelting him and his partner with bottles and bricks. Charlie managed to get the shotgun from the car. He fired a few rounds over the mob. People saw the fire spitting from the barrel and heard the booming of the shells going off.

Someone yelled, "Best to get your ass the hell out of here. That fool will kill you." Charlie was getting a reputation in that tough neighborhood as a cop who would shoot at the drop of a hat. It was funny to go on a call with him. People kept their distance from Charlie, and didn't take their eyes from his gun.

All that shooting at close range and Charlie never hit anyone. Another day he was chasing an armed robber. They were about seventy-five yards apart.. The robber turned and fired at Charlie. Charlie fired one shot, hit the guy on the tip of his nose and dropped him. Seeing this, other officers teased Charlie. "You empty your gun at guys six feet away and can't hit them. Today you fire at seventy-five yards and hit the guy. Charlie, you're improving."

But the topper was a night when we got a call of a burglary in progress. When we pulled up, a guy jumped from a second-story window. Charlie and I chased him. The guy didn't realize he ran into a dead-end alley. Charlie shouted, "Come out of there."

Hearing Charlie's voice, the burglar came out and so did two other guys with their hands above their heads shouting, "Don't shoot, Officer Charlie." We never found out what the other two guys were doing in that alley.

CHAPTER 3
THE THING

Everyone had been waiting for it. The previews were scary. Now they could see the whole movie. People standing in line for tickets, read the large advertisement poster which read, *"The Thing,* will make the hair on your head stand up. Your teeth will chatter. If you have a weak heart, don't enter." Some people reading this, shook their heads and got out of line and walked away. Their friends coaxed them to come back. The excitement was building to the max.

A couple blocks away two teenage boys were on their way to the movie, talking about how good it was going to be. Mark, the taller of the two, bent over and beckoned a large cat to come to him. "Here kitty, here kitty." The cat slowly walked to him and he picked it up and petted it. The cat loved it and stayed still and purred. The other boy Steve shouted, "Put that damn cat down, I want to get to the show." Mark kept petting the cat and caught up to Steve.

"Mark, what'cha you going to do with that cat?"

"The cat wants to see the movie too. I'm sure he'll enjoy it."

"You're nuts! You can't take that cat inside. They won't let you in."

"Don't worry about it. This cat will get to see the show."

The two boys got into the ticket line. Before it was Mark's turn to purchase his ticket he put the cat inside his coat.

The movie was almost sold out. There were hardly any seats left when they walked down the aisle. Finally they saw two. The people stood up to let the boys get to the vacant seats. Steve and Mark took their coats off and sat down. Steve shook his head. "Man, what the hell is the matter with you bringing that damn cat in here? You nuts?"

Mark kept petting the cat that now was in his lap. "Just don't mind him nice cat, we're going to have some fun."

The house lights dimmed! The screen lit up. The people were silent. It seemed they were too scared to talk. Fifteen minutes passed and everyone was on the edge of their seats. Their eyes were focused at the screen. It was the part where the monster was about to appear. Mark leaned forward and put the cat on the floor. In a soft voice he said, "Go take a nice walk big cat."

The cat slowly crawled under the seats. Mark elbowed Steve. "Watch! You'll be able to see right where the cat is." He no sooner said it when a man five rows down jumped up and yelled, "Yeooow, what the hell was that?" The cat must of got frightened because he let out a loud screech.

A woman a couple seats away from the man climbed onto her seat screaming, "I felt it. I felt it. It's inside with us."

Some one else yelled, "Damn, it's in here. It's crawling under the seats." People rushed into the aisles and ran out the exits. The house lights went on.

****

"Unit four, go to the Ohio theater there's a panic going on. When you get there keep us informed."

"Unit Four OK"

CHAPTER 4
PECKING ORDER

As I walked up to the house, I could hear loud music and laughing. Helen met me at the front door. Immediately, she grabbed my arm and pulled me into the front room where the party was going full blast. She threw up her arms and shouted, "Quiet! Quiet!" Everyone settled down and stared at her. She pointed at me and said, "You better pay attention. Bob here is a cop. If you get drunk, or misbehave, he'll arrest you."

My pulse rate shot up, and my face turned red. I sheepishly looked around the room and all eyes were fixed on me. At a loss for words, I nodded my head and shrugged my shoulders. I threaded my way through the staring people and went into the kitchen where the refreshments were. I thought, I'll be leaving this party in a short time. If I don't, the rest of the night will be talking police work.

I got a drink and was munching on some chips when a middle-aged man came up. He was smiling, "She got you this time."

I squinted and asked, "What?"

"The introduction. The last time she introduced me as Doctor Bennet. The rest of that night all I heard were peoples' ills. It ruined the party for me. Before I left that night I told her that if she ever introduced me as a doctor again, I would never attend another one of her parties. Tonight she didn't spot me. She spotted you."

I agreed and said, "Sometimes you just like to get away from the job. Just sit back like an ordinary person an relax and enjoy yourself."

He put out his hand and we shook. "I'm Mike, what's your name?"

"Glad to meet you, Mike, I'm Bob. I promise not to tell you my ills if you don't mention police work." We both laughed.

The doctor knew about life and had a great sense of humor. He cocked his head back, "Did you ever notice, Bob, when you first meet someone they don't ask your name? They always say, 'What do you do for a living?' Humans are just like chickens. They want to know where they stand in the pecking order."

"Bob, I'm going to tell you a story where I almost caused a disturbance on a plane because of what we're talking about. I was flying out of Detroit for California. I took a seat by the window and put my briefcase on my lap in hopes of catching up on some back work. A little old lady sat next to me. She immediately said, 'I'm flying to California to see my son. He's a famous lawyer. He has a five hundred thousand-dollar home.'

I looked at her and said. "That's nice." I noticed she was wearing some very expensive clothes.

She went on, 'My husband owns his own business and he made it big.' I realized she was working the pecking order in reverse. It would just be a matter of time and she'll be asking me the magic question. *What do you do for a living?* I tried to be kind and kept saying that's nice while all the time I was thinking what I was going to tell her when she asked what I did for a living. If I told her, I was a doctor she would ask for cures for her, her relatives and her friends. She wouldn't stop talking until we got to California. I'd never get anything done.

Her conversation continued concerning the achievements of her family. She finally hesitated and her eyes looked over her glasses and said. 'And what do you do for a living?'

I looked over my shoulder pretending I didn't want anyone else to hear what I was about to say. I than stared into her eyes and said. "I'm a pimp."

She didn't move. She gasped. "You're aha-a what?"

"I'm a pimp."

She quivered, grabbed her overnight bag and ran to the stewardess. She pointed at me and kept talking fast. The stewardess patted her back and calmed her down. She got her another seat in the rear of the plane. When the stewardess passed out the food she quickly put mine down and gave me a funny look.

Back in the kitchen I was laughing so hard I sprayed pieces of chips from my mouth. It took some time to get my composure. I wiped my eyes and a lady was standing in front of me with a serious look. She blurted out. "The other day I got a ticket for running a red light at 4[th.] and Main. The cop wouldn't listen to me when I tried to tell him something was wrong with the traffic light." The doctor who was standing behind her smiled, winked, and nodded.

CHAPTER 5
SHORT ENGAGEMENT

Louie Monto and Maggie Morgan graduated from the police academy on the same day.

Most of Louie's career was as a detective working the midnight shift. Maggie worked in uniform, then in the Crime Prevention Bureau on days. They hardly saw each other during the thirty-three years they were on the department. The day they retired, both showed up at the supply sergeant's office to turn in their equipment.

Maggie came in after Louie, and she laughed. "I guess we're the dinosaurs of our class. Everyone else has retired."

"You're right, Maggie. Man. Those years went by fast. I can still remember walking the beat when we first came on. What's your plans, Maggie?"

"Oh, I'll just rest for a couple of weeks and see what comes up. No set plans."

"Well, best of luck. I'm headed south. There will never be another snow flake hit this old body."

Maggie laughed. "You have a good time."

Louie nodded at her and went out the door. After walking down the empty hallway, he stopped and looked back at the door to the supply room. He waited for Maggie to come out.

She walked up to him. "What's the matter, did you forget something?"

"No, I was thinking. They say that this retirement can be lonely. Do you think you're going to be lonely?"

"I don't know. What are you getting at?"

"Well, let's not take a chance. Why don't we get married

and go south together?"

Maggie looked startled, then said, "Why not?"

"Okay, what you say I come to your house tonight and we'll make plans?"

"That's all right with me. Do you know where I live?"

"No, tell me."

"1210 Ontario Street. How about seven?"

"That's great. I'll see you then."

Two days later Louie went to the Homicide Bureau where he used to work. He walked up to his old partner, Stan Stager, who was typing a report. Stan looked up. "Hey Louie, what's the matter? You lonesome? That retirement isn't all it's cracked up to be, huh?"

"No, it's not that."

Stan could tell something was bothering him. "Hey, Louie, what the hell is going on with you? Come on, let it out."

Louie looked at the other detectives to make sure they weren't listening. "Stan, I'm going to get married."

Stan shouted. "You're what?"

"Hold it down, Stan, we don't want this to get around. We just want a quiet ceremony in Judge Andrew's chambers, then we're sneaking out of town. We want you to stand up for us."

"Yeah, sure. Who are you marrying?"

"Maggie Morgan."

"Maggie Morgan, the cop who worked Crime Prevention? How long have you and her had something going?"

"It was just a spur of the moment thing."

"You mean you never took her out on a date and you're marrying her?"

"Yeah, you can say that. Like I said, it's no big deal. We just want a quiet ceremony. Will you stand up for us? It's tomorrow at three thirty."

"You know I will. I'd be proud to do it for you."

"Thanks a lot, Stan. I'll have a boutonniere delivered to you in the morning. I'll see you at three-thirty in Judge Andrew's chambers. Thanks a lot, Stan. Remember keep it quiet."

"Sure Louie, see you tomorrow."

The next day Stan got the boutonniere and pinned it on his jacket. It wasn't long before the rest of the squad asked what the flower was about. He tried to keep it a secret but slowly the other detectives got it out of him. It wasn't long before the detectives who were all friends of Louie were in a huddle, whispering and laughing.

The ceremony was nice and Judge Andrew said, "Kiss the bride."

Louie hesitated then kissed Maggie for the first time. Judge Andrew shook their hands and wished them luck. He opened the door and they were startled. Standing on both sides of the hallway were at least thirty uniform policemen facing each other with latex gloves on holding their billy clubs over their heads forming an arch for the newly weds to walk under.

Louie looked at Stan and mumbled, "You rotten son-of-a-bitch."

"Louie, listen to me, I had nothing to do with this. Believe me, I would never do something like this."

The bride, groom, Stan and the lady who stood up for them quickly left the building and ran to Louie's car to go to a nice restaurant. The uniformed officers followed and stood on the steps of the Safety Building and watched as the car pulled away from the curb. Everyone of them burst out laughing when the tin cans that were hidden under the car and tied to the back bumper started dancing making all kinds of racket. Another officer who was hiding behind a tree, quickly caught up with the car and stuck a large sign on the trunk - "Just Married." Stan who was driving got caught up in the celebration and started blowing the horn. People walking on the sidewalks waved. Other cars blew their horns wishing the newlyweds luck.

Louie looked at Maggie, shrugged his shoulder and they both laughed.

* * * *

Fifteen years later, Louie and Maggie are still happily married.

CHAPTER 6
CON MAN

The voice of the dispatcher crackled over the radio, "Four Patrol. Two men fighting at Galena and Superior in front of the Plaza Bar." Four Patrol acknowledged and the red lights and siren were activated. On arrived at the scene the officers jumped from the paddy wagon and untangled the two combatants who were rolling around on the sidewalk. One officer shouted, "Break it up. What's going on here?" Even though the officers had the fighters in head-locks, they kept trying to get at each other.

The younger fighter shouted, "He started it. He's a damn con artist." The officers told him to quit yelling and slow down. The man took a deep breath and unraveled his story.

He pointed at the tavern. "I was in that bar minding my own business. This bum came in and sat next to me. He struck up a conversation, and started his con. He took off his hat and held it in front of me. He says, 'I'll bet you a beer you can't jump over it.' I took him up on it.

He stood and walked to the corner of the room where the walls meet and dropped his hat in that corner. No way could I jump over that hat unless I knocked one of the walls down. I told him he won and I bought him a beer. We drank a few more and he says, 'Want to get even? I'll bet you double or nothing I can do something you can't.'

I thought I was younger and a better man so I said okay. Now you won't believe what the fool did. He took out his glass eye and dropped it in his beer and chugged the glass dry, then put his eye back in his head. He smiled and said, 'Your turn.' I gagged and shook my head. I bought him two more beers.

The old crook then said, 'I never seen you before, right?'
I said right. I never saw you before.

'Well I got your name tattooed on my ass. Want to bet ten
bucks? I couldn't believe he knew my name so I put my ten
bucks on the bar and he pulls down his pants and tattooed on
his butt is, *Your Name*. I paid him again.

He kept it up for about an hour. He was pissing me off and
getting on my nerves. I wanted to punch him, but I didn't. He
knew he had me all worked up and he comes up with this
gimmick. He says, 'I'll bet you twenty-five dollars I can kick
harder than you.'

I told him to explain. He laughed, 'We'll see who can take
the most pain. We'll take turns kicking each other in the front
part of the leg between the ankle and the knee. Whoever stops
first, loses.' Well, this was better than punching him. I knew I
could win this one.

We both stood up and faced each other. He yelled, 'You
go first.' I kicked him as hard as I could and the old fool didn't
flinch. He kicked me, and it hurt like hell, but I didn't show
any pain. I gave it all I had and kicked him again. He laughed
and kicked me so hard I had to bend over. He shouted, 'Had
enough, Punk?' I told him hell no, and kicked him again. This
kicking went on until my foot caught the cuff of his pants. His
pant leg went up and I saw he had a wooden leg. He tried to
make me pay him twenty-five dollars. I told him, no way
because he tricked me and I wasn't going to pay him anymore
That's when the fight started."

The young fighter pulled up his pants and exposed his leg.
"Look officers my leg is swollen from the ankle up because of
that old fool." He glared at the con man and lunged at him. "I
oughta' wring your neck like they do old chickens."

The officers cooled the man down. They gave the fighters
a choice, leave or jail. The combatants walked away in
opposite directions. One was limping. The officers watched
them and shook their heads.

CHAPTER 7
STEPPIN' OUT DUDS

Tonight was the night. The big dance. Sadie and Leroy were excited. They waited two months and it finally arrived. Even though Sadie weighed two hundred and seventy-five pounds, she looked nice all dressed up. Leroy was five foot six and weighted a hundred and thirty pounds. He looked her over and shook his head. "Woman, you sure look fine."

Sadie smiled. "Leroy, you look so sharp in your suit. The cleaners did a good job. We sure are going to have a nice time tonight. I can't wait."

Leroy opened the door for her when they left the house. He hadn't done that for a long time. He patted her on the behind. "Yes sir'ee, we sure are going to have a good time. Everything is going to be cool. There'll be no problems, baby." She nodded and bent over and kissed him on top of his head. He looked up at her and smiled.

Leroy opened the door again for Sadie when they entered the dance hall. She smiled at him and grabbed his hand. Their bodies swayed with the music as they walked to their table. People shouted compliments at the happy couple. Sadie and Leroy smiled and waved back.

Leroy grabbed Sadie's chair and pulled it away from the table. She dropped down on it. Leroy strained to push the chair closer to the table. He tapped her on the shoulder. "Damn, Baby, you gotta' stand up. I can't budge it." She leaned onto the table and he pushed the chair in. He quickly ran to the other chair across from Sadie and sat down, then reached across the table and took her hands and gazed into her eyes. They looked at each other with deep affection. Words were not necessary. They were in ecstasy.

"Hey, Leroy, let me do some steppin' with your woman." The trance was broken.

Leroy squinted, hesitated, then said, "Yeah, yeah, sure, Fred." Fred got behind Sadie's chair and tried to pull it away from the table. He wrestled with it but it wouldn't budge. Sadie managed to stand up and he pulled the chair out. Fred and Sadie walked to the dance floor and soon disappeared in the crowd of dancers. Leroy started drinking and waiting.

Many songs went by and Fred escorted Sadie back to the table. Fred bowed and smiled. "Thanks, Sadie, you sure got some great moves. And thank you, Leroy." Leroy didn't answer, he just stared into his glass.

Sadie sensed something was wrong. She reached over to get Leroy's hand. He pulled away. "What's the matter with you, Leroy?"

Silence, then Leroy blurted out, "Listen, Bitch, I said a dance, not five. You made me feel like a fool sitting here by myself and all my friends staring and talking about me. I ought to reach over there and slap you up side that big ugly fat head."

Sadie didn't hesitate. She jumped up with her fists clenched. "Whose head you going to slap. You skinny little sapsucker. I'll break your puny ass in half."

Leroy got up so quick his chair fell over. He was ready to fight until he looked at her new dress. Pointing at the door, he shouted. "Come on you sorry fat-ass-bitch, let's get out of here and settle this mess at home."

She stared at his suit then looked down at her dress. "Okay. You nasty little bastard.

Let's get home. I can't wait." She turned and ran out the door. He followed right behind her, yelling. People stared and couldn't understand what was happening.

When the car stopped in front of their home, Sadie rushed out and ran to her bedroom. She hung her new dress on a hanger and put on a pair of old jeans and a sweat shirt, all the time cussing. In no time she was in the front yard yelling. "Where you at, you skinny little punk? You ain't talking shit like that to me. I'm going to whomp you into tomorrow."

"I'm over here you elephant ass bitch." They charged each other and the battle was on.

****

"Unit 9, 1202 Yates Street man and woman fist-fighting in the front yard. Step it up, sounds like a good one."

The scout car pulled up with red lights flashing. The two officers ran to the battling couple. A large woman was choking a small man. The little guy was punching her in the stomach. One of the officers shouted, "Break it up. What's going on here?" The couple kept battling. The officers managed to pull them apart. Leroy and Sadie saw the officers and quickly quieted down. Leroy put up his hands and explained what had happened at the dance.

The officers looked puzzled. One of them asked, "You mean this started at the dance hall and you came all the way home to fight?"

Leroy nodded. "You see, officers, we were dressed in our good clothes. We didn't want to tear them in a fight so we came home and changed into our old clothes to settle this mess."

The officers looked at each other and shook their heads. One of them asked, "Is it settled? Is there going to be any more trouble?"

Leroy shook his head. "No, officers, everything is cool. The fight is over. There will be no more trouble." Saddie nodded. The large woman and the small man put their arms around each other and walked into their house.

The officers stared at them and shook their heads.

CHAPTER 8
PAYBACK

The rookie police officer stared in horror at the beaten young woman lying on the gurney. Her once attractive face was scarred, her lips, swollen and lacerated; nose, distended and bloody; eyes purple and puffed shut. Deep welts oozed blood criss-crossed her body. He could see it hurt for her to cry as she suffered her pain in tiny sobs, clutching her hands over broken ribs where she hurt the most.

"What happened, Miss, who beat you like this? What did he use?" The doctor asked, shaking his head.

Her eyes opened to a bare slit. "Car antenna," she rasped weakly.

"Who did this to you, lady," the young officer shouted in outrage, trying hard to control his anger, " What kind of savage kicked you around like this?"

The young girl turned away, refusing to answer. The officer turned in frustration to his partner, a man much older and almost ready for retirement. "She won't say a damn thing. What's the matter with her? Doesn't she realize we wanna' help?"

"Sure, sure, Danny, but she's a whore and a junkie. Now listen to me, boy. Make out your report and say she won't tell who did it. Finish. No investigation, no prosecution." With a look of resignation he turned away.

"Hey, wait a minute, Eddie, that girl is beat bad! I don't care what or who she is. No one has a right to punch her around like that!"

Eddie shrugged. "Let me tell you straight out, you have no

choice. Her pimp beat her up and she'll never snitch. Did you look at her arms? The needle marks? That bitch will do anything for him, just to get another fix. Danny, you're wasting your time trying to make her squeal on her man."

His words only seemed to incense the young officer. "I wanna' get that bastard!" He leaned over the girl, close to her ear. "Listen, you gotta' understand, he had no right to do this, just tell me his name. I'll throw his ass in jail. No one has the right to do this to you."

His partner distanced himself and started to walk away. "I wish you luck, but I'm not wasting my time. I'll be out in the car when you're finished."

"Just give me his name," the young officer persisted. "I promise you I'll get him."

The painful mumbled whisper was said with great effort. "Please, let it go. Please, you can't help me."

Danny gazed at her arms and saw the marks. *How can girls do this to themselves. What reduces them to wallow in such a life of misery and repeated abuse? Beaten and trampled down, the poor kid thinks she has to take this shit. What kind of low life feeds off these helpless vulnerable victims.* "For God's sake," he yelled, "You've got to tell me. Next time he'll kill you for sure. I'll never forgive myself if he does. Tell me, please."

It was an effort to move her swollen lips. "Leave me alone, let it go."

Feeling defeated, he remained standing when the attendant wheeled the gurney into the emergency room. Deeply upset over the incident, he walked to the car.

"Any luck?" His partner asked.

"Not a damn thing," the young officer answered, turning to look out the window.

"Look, Danny. I don't like to say 'I told you so, but you've got to learn about the whore and pimp relationship, weird as it is. He takes all the money, she takes all the risks and he kicks her ass besides." The veteran officer nodded his head in the direction of the carport adjacent to the emergency room. "See that violet Cadillac with all the chrome? The guy sitting behind the wheel is her pimp."

The rookie officer jumped out of the car and ran to the Cadillac. He banged on the window for the guy to open it. As he glanced at the fender he noticed the car antenna had been broken off. Slowly the window rolled down. "Hey, what's your problem, man, the bitch didn't talk so shove off!" He gave a cocky smirk and started to roll up the window.

"Hold it, you bastard, I'm not done." He reached into the window and grabbed the pimp by the neck, but his partner was already there, holding the young officer back.

"Turn him loose, Danny, goddamn, turn 'im loose," he yelled, pulling him away from the Cadillac. "Now get back into our car." Danny pointed an angry finger at the pimp as he reluctantly backed away. "Why the hell did you maul that young girl, you hurt her worse than a wild beast, you goddamn scum, you!"

The pimp smiled and was about to fling an insult when the older officer stopped him with a look brimming with hate. "I wouldn't advise it," he urged, "Get the hell outta' here!"

* * * *

Months passed and the incident was obscured by other cruel beatings on women. Danny realized there was nothing he could do without a formal complaint, but it went against his sense of decency and honor to accept as inevitable the senseless and cruel abuse inflicted upon such helpless women who, tied to their pimp by the addiction to drugs, were dragged down to the lowest forms of humanity.

One day, Danny's partner pointed to a car. "Over there, by the bar, the pimp's bar, see that violet Cadillac? Look familiar?"

"That goddamn pimp! But we can't get anything on the bastard. When I think what he did to that girl."

"Listen, I got an idea." Eddie drove down an alley and pulled out the knife he always carried. "Danny, see that clothesline over there? Cut it and bring it here. Don't ask questions."

Dan did as he was told and handed the line over to his

partner. Meanwhile Eddie picked up a metal garbage can from the alley and placed it in the back seat. They drove off and parked close to the Cadillac. Eddie got out and tied one end of the rope to the back bumper of the Cadillac. He then stretched out the rope and tied the other end to the metal garbage can. Carefully, concealing the rope, he placed the garbage can on the sidewalk as though it belonged there. He got back into his vehicle, made a U-turn and headed down the block.

With a puzzled look, Danny waited for an explanation.

Eddie grinned. "Now we wait."

A short time later, the pimp came out with two of his girls. He barked out orders to his pitiful victims who dutifully listened, then went back to the bar to solicit more business. The older officer peered through his field glasses. "There he is, that slime, relieving his girl-slaves of their money, threatening them, making sure they don't cheat. He'll make a few more pickups from his broads, then he'll go out and splurge on a big meal and go shopping for more sharp clothes. Goddam bastard, makes me wanna' puke."

Danny could see his partner was becoming progressively angry, his fury mounting. "So, what's gonna' happen when he drives away with the garbage can dragging behind his car?"

"The pimps and guys around here, love their cars. Just wait. I'm sure justice will be served."

Eddie got out of the scout car and went to a pay phone. He dialed the number and a voice said, "Flame Bar, who you want?"

"Let me speak to Big Man."

"This is Big Man."

"Man, I'm over at the Adam Street Bar. One of yo' hos' is higher then hell. She be spending all her money buying drinks for these thirsty dudes."

"She what? That bitch best not be spending my money, I'll be right there."

Eddie walked back to the scout car. "Now the fireworks is about to happen."

The pimp came running out of the bar. He drove off with

tires squealing and the can trailing. It hit a pot-hole and took flight, bouncing off the hood of a shiny Buick. The owner, a stocky man, was entering a carry-out when he heard the loud bang. He quickly turned and saw the garbage can rebound off the hood of his car, bounce to the roof, scratching and nicking its way along the shiny blue paint. Raising his fist, he screamed curses and threats. He jumped in his car and chased the culprit.

The can again struck the street and zig-zagged wildly over a new red number, another pimp's car. A group of teens, admiring their cars parked on the street in front of a car wash, recoiled in disbelief when the can glanced recklessly off their cars causing large dents. Shouting obscenities they jumped into their cars like firemen answering a call and gave chase to the violet Cadillac, with wild revenge in their eyes.

With a grin, the older officer put down the field glasses. He waited a moment then turned on the overhead red lights and siren. "I guess it's time to come to the scumbag's rescue."

The pimp was already on the ground, unfortunately not yet badly hurt, although his face was bruised and his clothes were torn, and the pockets to his pants ripped out. "Man, am I glad to see you guys, those cats were goin' t'kill me, they said I tore up their rides." He got up and turned away from the threatening glares of the men who stood with clenched fists.

Danny shouted. "You wanna' prosecute? Make 'em serve jail time? Let's walk over, get their names and addresses so we can get warrants for their arrests."

The pimp shook his head. "Man, I jes' wanna get my ass out of here and forget this scene. I can't understand this shit, man, them cats are crazy," he mumbled under his breath.

Danny walked over to the men. "Any you guys wanna' prosecute this guy for malicious destruction of property?"

They looked mad, still steaming from the attack of the garbage can to their cars. One of them spoke, "Naw, we got our money from him."

"Well, then, let's everyone break it up. Glad you worked out the problem."

The pimp limped back to his car. He leaned on the fender.

Then he noticed the antenna he replaced had been broken off again. Getting off a few steamy phrases, he fell into the car seat. His eyes popped wide open when he saw the broken antenna woven into the steering wheel.

Danny was boiling. "Hey, Eddie, what the hell goes with you? You just stood by the pimp's car while I did all the talking. You hate those pimps worse'n I do, yet you never said a word to that slimy bastard, or any of 'em."

"Yeah," he sighed wearily, "Yeah, you're right, I can't stand them sons-of-bitches, but what you don't know, is if they said the wrong word, I don't think I'd be able to control myself.

Those pimps are the lowest form of life on earth, I'd like to exterminate 'em all with my bare hands!"

The older officer's head turned away. It was silent for a minute. "Listen, Danny, I'm going to tell you this and it is between me and you." His voice broke. "My daughter got herself mixed up with one of those bastards when she was only fourteen years old. A pimp ruined her life, as well as mine. Every time I drive along skid row, I try not to look for fear of seeing her walking the streets." He choked up and I felt my heart break for him.

Danny's partner Eddie retired and they lost touch. Then one day the police department was stunned by a gigantic explosion in the pimp's hangout. It made the headlines. There were no survivors. No one knew how it happened. It was then that Danny recalled the rest of the confidential conversation he had with Eddie that day when he set up the pimp's car.

"You know, kid, if the time ever comes after I retire - that I have a terminal illness - I'll tie ten sticks of dynamite to the lining of my coat. I'll walk into that pimps' nest and sit up at the bar right in the middle of them. I'll be real friendly like, even force a smile and order them drinks. Then I'd light the wick outta' the sleeve of my coat and offer a toast."

"Here's to you low life, slimy bastards, you're gonna' get a bang out of this!"

The case was never solved.

CHAPTER 9
MR. CLAZY MAN

Big Hank leaned back and took a deep breath after securing the tug to the dock. The storm last night on the lake was a mean one. He felt lucky bringing in the large freighter without an accident.

Hank was a big man, all of six three and two hundred and forty pounds. He's a man who keeps to himself, and likes it quiet. A John Wayne type.

It was early morning and Hank wanted to unwind. He walked into the first tavern that had an open sign on the door. It was deserted. He pulled a stool away from the bar with his foot and sat down. After waiting a few minutes he heard noise from the back room. A short stocky man with dark hair and a bushy mustache walked behind the bar and stood in front of Hank. He shouted in broken English. "Gooda' morning, Mr. Customer. Howa' you like mya' place. Nicea' place huh? What - cha' want?"

"I want a shot and a beer in clean glasses. I don't want to be shortchanged. I don't want any conversation because I don't understand a damn thing you're saying."

"What cha' mean, shorta' change?"

"I hope your math is better then your English. No stealing. You get it?"

The bar owner continued to stare then shrugged his shoulders and got the drinks.

An hour passed and not a word was exchanged. Every time Big Hank's glasses went dry he pointed at them and the owner refilled them.

Hank continued putting away the double shots, and beers. He looked at himself in the mirror behind the bar. He was in deep thought and the bar owner didn't disturb him. The front door opened. Hank didn't bother to look at who came in. The bar owner was filling Hank's glasses. He stopped and stared at the new arrival. His eyes opened wide and his lips started quivering.

Hank sensed something wrong. His eyes went back to the large mirror and waited for the reflection of the stranger. A man appeared. His head was covered by a pillow case with holes cut where his eyes peered out. He was holding a double barrel twelve gauge shotgun. He pointed the gun at the owner. "Hey, creep, give me all your damn money."

The owner didn't have any trouble understanding this conversation. His hands were in the air and his whole body trembled. "Okay, okay, don'ta' shoot thata' biga' gun. I givea' you everything. My money is your money."

Big Hank didn't like people who scare. He pointed at the owner. "Don't give that bum a penny." The owner was shaking and his eyes were as big as saucers.

The owner pointed at Hank. "Youa' damna' clazy man talking likea' that. Thisa' robber shoot me a dead with big gun. "Mr. Robber, you noa' listen to clazy man. Ia' give you everything Ia' got. Don'ta' shoot the biga' gun."

Hank slammed his fist down on the bar. "I said you don't give this phony anything. If you do I'll jump over this bar and kick your ass." The bar owner's eyes went from Big Hank to the shotgun. His lips quivered. He was cussing and praying in English and some foreign language at the same time. He turned and started to open the cash register. Big Hank yelled, "No!"

The robber shouted. "Shut up, big mouth or I'll blow your damn head off."

Big Hank yelled back. "I'll make you eat that damn gun."

The owner knew there was real trouble now. "Oh, a my. Oh, a my. I'm gonna get a big hole shot in me." In the mirror Big Hank saw the robber starting to point the gun at him. He jumped to his feet and at the same time grabbed the barrels of the shotgun and pulled upwards. Two loud explosions erupted and chunks of plaster and dust rained from the ceiling. Hank held the gun by the barrels like a baseball bat. He slammed it into the side of the robber's head breaking the stock off and sending the robber into a table with chairs stacked on top. The chairs flew like bowling pins and the robber dropped unconscious to the floor.

The bar owner yelled into the phone. "Pleasea' send lots of policemens. Man with a biga' gun. Clazy man get mea' killed, shoota' biga hole in my bar. Send help. Lotta' help. Buffalo Tavern - yes. Mya' place."

Big Hank walked back to his stool and threw the broken shotgun behind the bar. He sat down and slowly picked his drink up and looked at the mirror again.

Police cars pulled up. Covered with white dust the owner ran out the front door shouting. The officers squinted when they saw him. They tried to calm him, but he continued to scream in broken English. They could only understand, "Clazy man, big gun."

The officers entered the bar with their guns drawn. They pointed them at Big Hank who was still sitting at the bar. An officer shouted. "Hey, you, what's going on here?"

Big Hank continued to sit and stare at the mirror. He raised his hand and pointed over his shoulder with his thumb at the guy on the floor. "Ask him."

The owner re-entered the bar screaming. He pointed at the guy on the floor with the pillow case still over his head. "That Som Bitch come in witha' biga' gun and rob me." He then pointed at Hank. "That Clazy Som Bitch get mea' killed." He pointed to his cash register

"Thirty-fivea' dollar in register. Ia' givea him thirty- fivea' dollar and he go and noa' shoot. He pointed at the ceiling where half of it was blown out. "Fivea' hundred dollar get ita' fixed. He looked back at Big Hank. "Clazy somb bitch graba' big gun boom, boom mya' ceiling come down." He slapped the top of his head and a cloud of plaster dust erupted.

Three weeks passed and the officers who had been on the call at the Bufflo Tavern were talking about the subpoenas they received. One officer said, "Remember the bar where the guy took the shot gun away from the robber? The owner is suing him to pay for a new ceiling."

CHAPTER 10
POWERFUL STUFF

Willie reached into his pocket and pulled out all the change he had panhandled. He figured he had enough money to buy a bottle of cheap wine. Entering the store located on skid row he saw a sign. *Closeout sale. 3 bottles of Velvet Smooth Grape Wine $2.50.* He ran to the counter and threw his coins down.

The clerk watched the coins roll around. "What you going to have?"

Willie pointed at the sign. "Give me three bottles of that Velvet stuff or whatever you call it."

The clerk counted the change and looked up at Willie. "You're short a quarter."

Willie acted surprised. He threw another quarter on the counter. "Sorry about that man."

The clerk shook his head. He was used to this type of scam from guys like Willie. He bagged the three bottles. Willie snatched the bag and ran out the door.

Willie walked as fast as he could to the river bank and laid down in some high weeds. He unscrewed the cap and raised the bottle to his mouth.

About fifty yards away two young boys were target shooting with a twenty-two-caliber rifle. One of them saw the bottle raise from the weeds. He pointed at it and said to his friend, "Jim, lets see if you can hit that bottle." Jim took careful aim and fired.

Willie was waiting for the liquid to run down his throat. Instead the bottle exploded showering him with wine and broken glass. Frightened, he shouted, "Damn." He grabbed the bag with the two remaining bottles and ran to a condemned vacant house where he had been staying. He climbed the creaking steps to the attic where he couldn't be seen by anyone. He carefully reached into the bag and took out another bottle. He turned his head and closed his eyes as he slowly unscrewed the cap. He waited a minute and cautiously brought the bottle to his lips. He watched the bubbles shoot up as the wine drained from the bottle down his throat. After every drop was gone he burped, wiped his mouth with his shirt sleeve and fell asleep.

Early the next morning a large crane with a clamshell positioned itself in front of the dilapidated house.

Willie woke up in the attic with a bad hangover and the shakes. He reached into the bag and grabbed the remaining bottle. He was raising it to his lips when the whole roof of the house came off. Again he shouted, "Damn." He didn't use the rickety steps to get out of there. He jumped through the large hole in the roof. The operator of the crane was startled when he saw a man jump from the hole he just made with the clamshell.

Willie ran into the store where he bought the wine. The clerk knew there was going to be trouble when he saw Willie's expression. Willie shouted, goddamn it, man, what kind of crap was in them bottles? That shit exploded. You trying to kill me?" He jumped over the counter with his fists clenched.

"Unit 11, go to 120 Hawley St. Happy Party Store. Man attacking the store clerk."

CHAPTER 11
PISTOL PACKIN' GERTRUDE

Eighty-year-old Gertrude weighed one hundred pounds and stood five foot four. She took a chair in the front row of the hall. Senior citizens groups had made arrangements for a police officer to give instructions on how an elderly woman could defend herself.

The uniformed officer gave a short presentation, then started telling how items women carry on their person can be turned into weapons. He showed them car keys inserted between the fingers and then the hand rolled up into a fist with the keys protruding, a hat pin used as a puncturing weapon, high heeled shoes pushed into the groin of an assailant.

Gertrude listened but thought keys, hat pins and high heeled shoes were good advice for a younger woman but not for her. A gun would be the perfect weapon. It would speak for itself. As long as you're going to defend yourself get something that would do the job. She left the meeting and drove immediately to a pawn shop.

She bent over with her hands resting on the glass display case. She peered down at the guns. A large stainless steel revolver caught her eye. She thought if anyone tried anything, that would do the job.

A clerk walked up from behind the counter and stared down into the gray hair. "Can I help you?"

Gertrude looked up at him. "Yes, I want to buy that big silver gun."

"Are you buying this gun for yourself?"

"Yes, I want that gun. There's a lot of crazies out there

and I want to protect myself."

The clerk shook his head. "Lady, that's a three-fifty-seven magnum. It's a heavy gun and is very powerful. I suggest you get a smaller gun like a twenty-two or a thirty-two caliber. They are small and easy to handle."

"No, I want that big one. If I need to use it I want something that will do the job. Let me see that big one."

The clerk shook his head and reluctantly reached into the case and pulled out the large gun. He placed it on a rubber mat on top of the counter.

Gertrude grabbed the gun with both hands and slowly raised it so she could see through the sights. She closed one eye and opened the other one wide. The gun was shaking but she managed to hold it up in front of her. The clerk ducked. "Lady, don't aim that gun at me!"

She put the gun down on the mat. "Now listen, lady, that gun is too heavy for you. When you fire that gun it will kick like hell. Are you sure you want a powerful weapon like that?"

"Never mind all that talk. I want to see if it fits in my purse. If it fits I'm going to buy it." She unzipped her large purse and grabbed the gun. She managed to get it inside. "I'll take it. Now get me some bullets and show me how to load it."

The clerk reached behind him and pulled a box of shells from a shelf. He took six bullets out and put them on the counter. Gertrude handed him the gun. He released the cylinder and slid the bullets into the chambers. "You see the size of these bullets? There's going to be an enormous kick when you pull that trigger." He then started to unload it.

"Never mind the kick. Don't take the bullets out. I want it ready to go." She grabbed the loaded gun and put it in her purse.

"Lady, just remember one thing. When you fire that gun and it knocks you on you know what, don't come back complaining."

"Don't worry, me and Big Tom here are going to get along just fine."

From that day on Big Tom accompanied Gertrude every place she went. She never felt so safe. When she paid for something she'd open her purse wide. Store clerks' jerked backwards on seeing the large gun. Their eyes opened wide.

One day she left the supermarket with a cart of groceries. She rolled it to her car. She squinted when she saw three men inside. She didn't hesitate. She dropped her purse on the ground and pulled out the large revolver. She aimed it at the guy sitting behind the steering wheel. "You bums get the hell out of my car or I'll shoot." The man behind the wheel turned and looked down the barrel of the large gun and the old lady aiming it at him. Her hands were shaking and both her eyes were shut. Her finger was on the trigger.

"Aw, man, don't shoot, lady. Let me the hell out of here." He turned and scrambled out the passenger side door following his two friends.

Gertrude kissed Big Tom and returned it into her purse. She put her groceries onto the backseat and took out her car keys. She tried to get the ignition key in the slot but it wouldn't fit. She was getting ready to ask someone for help when she looked down the parking lane and noticed another car exactly like hers. She quickly returned her groceries to the cart and wheeled it to that car. She placed her groceries into this car and got behind the wheel and put the key in the ignition switch. It turned and the car started. She sat there for a moment looked at the other car, shrugged her shoulders and drove off.

CHAPTER 12
THE PREACHER

A group of iron workers sat at the bar exchanging jokes, relaxing and buying each other drinks after work. They were enjoying themselves. A thin man about thirty-five years old, six feet tall, wearing a faded blue suit, stained white shirt and a cheap necktie walked in and slammed the door. The men quickly turned and looked at the stranger then turned back to talk to their friends.

The stranger walked to the bar and as he passed the iron workers he reached in between them and stood a forty-five caliber bullet on the bar in front of them. The men looked confused. The stranger in the faded suit took a seat at the head of the bar.

Everyone watched him when he stood up and placed a briefcase on the bar. While he was opening it, he stared from one man to another. Not a word was said by the iron workers as they studied every move the stranger made. The man pulled a Bible from the briefcase. He raised it over his head and slammed it down. Everyone in the bar jumped. He opened the Bible and held it in his left hand. His right hand stayed in the briefcase. He shouted, "Hear me, sinners. Don't none of you move or you're gonna meet your maker. You heathens, should be home with your wives and children. What are you doing in this den of iniquity? You better repent. I'm here to save you. If I can't save you, I'll send you to the fires of hell. Put down those drinks. Alcohol is the ticket to Hell."

Ben, a large construction worker, still wearing his metal helmet, whispered to his friend sitting next to him. "I'm going to kick his ass and throw him out on his head."

His friend shook his head and said in a low voice, "Watch this guy Ben, he's a whacko. I bet he's got a gun in that briefcase. Don't do anything."

"Dispatcher, this is Sergeant Three. We have the Rooster Bar under observation. We believe a man inside is holding people hostage. Do we have a detective in the area. We need a plain clothes officer to go inside and find out the situation."

"Dispatcher, this is Unit Eight-Twelve, I'm two blocks away from the Rooster Bar. I'm not in uniform, I'll give them a hand."

"This is the Dispatcher; go and assist, Unit Eight-Twelve."

The crews were about a half block away from the bar. I pulled up and Sergeant Dowling came to my car.

"Bob, we got a guy in the bar who we think has a gun and is holding everyone hostage. Will you act like a customer and go inside and find out what's going on? If we go in there with uniforms, he might start shooting."

I pulled down my tie, messed up my hair, unzipped my fly and pulled out part of my white shirt than staggered to the front door. I opened it by shoving my shoulder into it. It banged open as I stumbled in. I slurred in a loud voice. "Give everybody a drink on me. I won big at the race track." I staggered to the juke box and shouted, "Bartender, turn up the volume. I want to hear my favorite songs." I dropped three quarters into the money slot. A forty-five caliber cartridge bounced off the juke box and dropped to the floor. A man at the end of the bar pointed a Bible at me and shouted..

"Lucifer, don't you play that noise from hell. Pull the plug to that sin-machine."

I looked at the men sitting at the bar and from their frightened looks, I thought I better do as he said. I pulled the plug and stared at him.

"Come here, Lucifer, sit next to me. You need to hear what I have to say more than these wicked sinners."

I took the seat next to him and tried to look inside his briefcase. It was no use. He had the cover down, concealing what he was holding in his right hand.

The preaching went on for about a half hour. Whenever someone nodded, or looked away from him, he would slam the Bible down and shout.

Every man in the place gave his complete attention to the guy screaming with his hand in the briefcase. All at once the preacher laid the Bible on the bar. He shouted at the bartender, "Get me a shot of whiskey with a beer wash, my mouth is dry from all this preaching." He now had both hands in the briefcase. Everyone leaned back ready to dive under a table fearing he was about to pull out a gun and start shooting. Instead, both his hands came out of the briefcase holding a Playboy Magazine. He raised it above his head showing the centerfold of a naked woman. He laughed and shouted, "Hey, boys, look at the boobs on this bitch. How'd you like to get some of this?"

I saw my chance, both his hands were exposed above his head. I grabbed his wrists, put my leg behind his and pushed his chest with my shoulder. Before he hit the floor, someone broke a beer bottle over his head. I sat on his chest holding his wrists. Feet were kicking him in the head and body from all directions. Men were yelling. "Beat that crazy bastard's ass."

I managed to get my badge out of my pocket. "Police, back off! I'll handle this." The front door flew open and blue-uniforms rushed in.

As I handcuffed the preacher I turned him over on his stomach. I pulled down the back of his shirt collar and printed on the inside in bold letters was - PATIENT TOLEDO MENTAL HOSPITAL. We searched his pockets and briefcase. There was no gun. We did find numerous pornographic books and a box of forty-five caliber bullets inside the briefcase.

We never found out how he got possession of the briefcase. I don't think the real owner wanted anyone to know who he was due to the material inside.

The preacher was transported back to the mental hospital.

CHAPTER 13
WHO'S SPITTIN' BEER

Old James sat in his wooden chair looking out the second story window of the cheap boarding house. It was a dark night and his eyes focused on the multicolored neon lights in front of the numerous bars down on the street. He thought, *Damn, here I sit, eighty years old and the only company I have are these four dreary walls. It seems like yesterday I was young and used to go into the taverns back in Tennessee and raise hell.*

The lights beckoned him to get out of the lonesome room. He went to the dresser and took out a clean flannel shirt. He got dressed and the next thing he knew he was walking down the bright street. He looked in a couple of the bars, there was hardly anyone inside. He wanted one that had people and action. His eyes focused on a large light going off and on and below it a sign, The Rumpus Room. He cupped his hands around his eyes and pressed them to the large window. It was crowded inside. People were laughing and singing. He mumbled to himself, "This is what I'm looking for."

He went in and sat at a table. In no time a waitress came. "What's it going to be, Pops?"

"Give me a big mug of beer."

Old James explored his surroundings. At the bar were two big construction workers wearing silver metal helmets. At the tables couples were talking and listening to the juke-box. The waitress placed a mug of beer in front of him. His fingers rubbed up and down the glass erasing the frosty moisture. His thoughts flashed back to his home town and the bar he used to go to. It must be fifty years since he was in that bar back in the hills. He smiled as he thought of how he used to take beer in his mouth and squirt it through his teeth and hit the red hot pot-bellied stove in the middle of the room. It made a loud sizzling noise and steam erupted. He must have done it a hundred times and never got caught. At his best he could hit that stove from fifteen feet away. This drove the bar owner crazy because he could never catch the guy.

James wondered if he could still do it. His tongue went to the roof of his mouth and he started counting teeth. There were only two left but they were the important ones. They were his front ones and the beer had to squirt between them. He looked around the room for a target. He picked one of the guys with the metal helmets. The man was shaped like the old pot-bellied stove. James took a big mouthful of beer. He positioned his tongue behind the liquid and started to force it to his two front teeth. He took a good aim at the helmet. His upper lip raised and a solid stream of beer shot out. James quickly brought the mug back to his mouth and looked in a different direction.

The stream of beer fell short and went into the man's ear. He jumped up and slapped at the side of his head and shouted. "Damn." He put his finger in his ear and then smelled it. He stood there for at least five minutes looking for the guy who did it. He finally sat down and started talking to his friend again. But every once in awhile he'd look over his shoulder.

Old James almost choked holding back his laughter. He knew if he laughed it would expose him. After a couple more beers, he got brave again. He felt proud. The old talent was still there. He looked around for another target. A heavy guy was sitting at a table with a girl. The back of his neck was so fat the rolls looked like hot dogs. James looked back to the bar at his first target with the metal helmet on. He thought, *I ought to try for a double banger.*

Old James again took a large mouthful of beer and primed it with his tongue. His upper lip raised and a straight stream of pressurized beer was on its way aimed at the neck of the fat guy sitting at the table. He quickly turned his head and shot another stream at the guy with the metal helmet. A splat and a ping sounded as the beer found its mark. Both guys jumped up wiping beer from their necks, cussing and looking around. They stared at each other. The guy with the metal helmet shouted, "So you're the wise guy. You like to play jokes, huh?" They ran at each other with clenched fists. Old James laughed.

James stopped laughing when he heard a woman shout. "Wait a minute, you guys. I saw the whole thing." She pointed at Old James. "That little guy sitting there, who looks like a rabbit, done it. He's the one who's spitting beer."

The men stopped and looked at James. James contemplated whether to run but he knew his old legs wouldn't carry him very far. The guy with the helmet was now standing at the table pointing at Old James. "You old coot, I ought a knock out them two teeth you got left so you'll never do it again."

A beat officer was outside and heard the commotion. He immediately went inside. Old James jumped up and got behind the officer. The officer asked the man with the helmet what happened. The guy explained. The officer escorted James from the bar. The old man looked up at him. "I promise officer I will never pull that stunt again. Just give me a break. There won't be any more trouble."

The officer smiled and walked Old James back to his boarding house.

CHAPTER 14
THE PILL

I was sorting my investigation reports out and going to work on the most serious crimes first. A couple of them looked interesting and I wanted to get started. A hand squeezed my shoulder. I looked up, Captain Barnes motioned with his finger. "Come into my office I want to talk with you." I got up and followed.

He pointed to a chair, "Have a seat."

I sat down and thought, what did I do? My mind did a quick rewind of the past couple of weeks. Even though I couldn't think of anything he might chew me out for, I was still uneasy. He was smiling. He knew what was going on in my head. He probably did some crazy things when he was a young officer.

"Bob, I got an assignment I want you to handle. I picked you because you worked with kids before. It will last a week. I want you to get on it right away."

"But Captain I just got a bunch of investigations this morning. I think I know a couple of suspects that did those crimes."

"Give them back to the assigning officer. I want you to work this one. If there's any problem tell him to come see me."

"Yes, Sir."

He tossed me a couple cellophane bags. Inside were brown pills the size of Alka Seltzers. "Bob, we got a problem with marijuana in our schools. Most of the teachers don't know what it looks or smells like. These pills in the bags are made from alfalfa and some other plant matter. When you put a lit match to them they smolder like a cigarette. The smell is exactly like marijuana. I want you to go to the schools and show the teachers how to recognize it.

"Yes, Sir." I walked out of his office with the simulators and went back to my desk. I opened up one of the bags and took out a pill. I rubbed it between my fingers and raised it to my nose. It had a mild odor like dry leaves. I studied it for a short time then reached over to the desk next to me and took an ashtray. I put a lit match to the pill and dropped it into the ashtray and immediately gray smoke billowed up. I smelled its sweet sickening odor. Half the pill glowed. I had enough of that stinking smell and grabbed my cup of stale coffee and extinguished the pill. Then I took the ash tray and rinsed it. The room reeked. I opened the windows even though it was cold outside.

Deputy Chief McAfee walked into the squad room. He took three steps and stopped abruptly. His nose wrinkled up as he sniffed. He went right to a detective who was smoking. He grabbed the detective's wrist and pulled it to his face and smelled the lit cigarette he was smoking. The startled detective jumped up. "What the hell's the matter with you? Are you nuts?"

I went to the schools and did what I was ordered to do. The smell of the pills nauseated me. It was unreal how much smoke came out of those small pills.

It was great not having to smell that rotten stuff when the assignment was done. The teachers were nice and polite, but I had to get back into the environment I was accustomed to. Give me those tough nuts that do crazy things.

After I got off work one night I went to Marty's Bar. It was a different type of bar. Most citizens in Toledo didn't want any part of Marty's. It was in a rough part of town. There was a strange relationship among the customers. Tough off-duty cops sat at one end of the bar. And ex-convicts and every other type of scoundrel sat at the other end. They all drank under the same roof. The cops liked it there because the hoodlums didn't bother them by asking stupid questions like, "How come you're drinking? You're a cop." The cops who went into Marty's were a group of men who worked the roughest part of the city. They did a good job. When they got off duty they didn't want to be bothered. The hoods knew this and left them alone. No one talked shop.

People didn't realize Marty's was probably the safest bar in town. One time, three armed bandits tried to rob the place. They pulled out their guns and shouted, "This is a hold up. Give us all your money." When the smoke cleared the robbers were dead on the floor. Investigators never determined how many bullets hit them. Word got out to other would-be robbers. There never was another robbery there.

I went into Marty's and sat at the cops' end of the bar. They nodded and didn't say much. Tables and chairs were being overturned behind me. I turned and two guys were pounding the hell out of each other. No one paid any attention. They didn't even look at the ruckus. I turned around and drank my beer.

I went to the head. On the way back I put my hand into my jacket pocket. I felt a familiar cellophane packet. I pulled it out and there were two simulators. I lit one of them and put it in an ashtray on top of an empty table and nonchalantly walked back to my stool at the bar. One of the off duty cops started sniffing. He looked at the other end of the bar. "One of them numb nuts down there is smoking pot." The other cops stared at the hoodlums. The hoodlums were looking at the cops.

An ex-con shouted, "Someone fired up some shit in here." I did everything I could not to laugh.

The smoke must have penetrated Marty's office. The door flew open and Marty ran out.

"Who the hell's smoking grass? No shit-smoking in my place. I don't want any more problems with Internal Affairs. Open the damn windows! Get that smell the hell out of here." He was now running up and down the bar examining everybody's cigarettes and ashtrays.

The open doors and windows flushed out the smell. After

the odor was gone they shut them.   Everything went back to normal.   I had a couple more beers and some conversation, then went to the juke box and played some songs.   On the way back to the bar, I took out the other simulator and lit it and put it in an ashtray.   I tapped a couple of the guys on the shoulders and said, "Well you guys, I got to get going.   Have a nice day."

CHAPTER 15
THE HOTTEST DAY EVER

It was the hottest day of the year. In the backroom of a pool hall sat six men huddled around a card table. Above their heads dangled a light with a funnel like shade. In the corner stood a large fan straining to make a breeze. The men resembled characters from, *The Godfather*. The owner of the pool hall who was winning, looked up at the other players. "What do you guys think? We've been playing for twenty-three hours. Maybe we should think about calling it quits."

Everyone looked up from their cards. Sam shouted, "Listen to him. He's winning big and he wants to quit. He don't wanna' give us a chance to get our money back."

Tony squirmed a little. "Now don't get me wrong. I'll play as long as you want to. I'll give you a chance to get your money back."

Big Ben continued to stare and pointed his finger. "You better." The only noise from then on was the shuffling of the cards.

A loud bang came from the front door. All heads turned to where the sound came from. Loud knocking again. Tony got up. "Who the hell is that?"

One of the players said, "Better hide the cards and money. The only guys who pound like that are the cops. Where's the backdoor?"

Tony shook his head. "Stay put, I'll see who it is." He walked through the pool hall and went to the large window. He slipped a finger into one of the slats of the Venetian Blinds. He shouted, "Don't worry you guys, it's just a couple of young punks." He opened the front door. "What the hell do you guys want?"

"We want to play pool. Why else would we be here?" They walked in.

Tony threw up his hands. "Get lost, we're not open."

The two young guys ignored him. "We came to play pool so get the hell out of our way."

"Listen, punks, the only pool you'll be playing is when I break this cue stick over your heads."

The young men stood defiantly with their fists clenched and were ready to make this dispute physical. The card players in the back heard the commotion and walked to the front of the pool room and stood behind Tony. The boys took one look at the reinforcements and slowly retreated. Tony slammed the door and locked it.

The players went to the backroom and resumed the card game.

The young men went across the street and sat on the curb staring at the pool room. Bill grabbed a brick and stood up. "I'm going to throw it right through that big front window."

Tim, the other boy shook his head. "You better not, Bill, those guys are tough and they're no one to fool with. They look like the mob. You'll be wearing cement shoes when they find you at the bottom of the Maumee River."

"I don't care how tough they are. I could take anyone of them." He stood with the brick contemplating whether to throw it. All at once he slammed the brick to the pavement. "I got a better idea. Come on, Tim, follow me."

Tim trailed behind Bill to the side of the pool hall. Bill bent down and opened the basement window and climbed in. He looked up at Tim, "Come on in, but be quiet. "

Tim climbed in and looked confused.. "What are we going to do now?"

"Go over there and get as much paper and wood as you can."

Tim did, and came back with arms full. Bill grabbed the paper and wood and stuffed them into the furnace. He struck a match and set it on fire. "Hurry, Tim, get more." Tim continued bringing the wood and paper and Bill kept throwing it on the fire. The flames roared. "Hurry, Tim, get that shovel and bring coal."

Tim brought shovels full and pitched it on the fire. Bill kept calling for more. Tim shouted, "That fire is hot enough. You'll burn the place down. I'm getting the hell out of here."

Bill grabbed the shovel and kept feeding more coal on the fire. Tim saw this and scrambled out the window and ran across the street and sat on the curb. In about five minutes Bill came out and ran up to him. "Now we just sit and wait."

Meanwhile, back in the poolroom, Tony pulled a handkerchief from his pocket and wiped large sweat beads from his forehead. "Man, I bet this is the hottest day ever."

Big Ben glared at him. "You want to quit again with your winnings?"

"No, man, I didn't mean it that way. It's hot. I never felt so warm."

About ten minutes passed and no conversation. Sam stood up and took off his shirt. Everyone followed suit. Tony wrapped his handkerchief around his head and tied it. "Man, I can never remember it being so hot. This place is like a steam bath."

One of the players shouted. "Quit talking and deal the cards."

The cards hit the table and Tony won another big pot. The men glared at him as he pulled in the winnings. Sam stood up and removed his trousers. The rest of them did the same. It was quite a sight seeing men sitting at the table bare-chested with only undershorts on. Tony saw the perspiration running down their faces. He ran behind the counter and got some towels and pitched them to the players. They quickly wiped their wet bodies.

The cards became soggy from the mens' wet hands. Sam jumped up and yelled, "I think I'm being cremated. I can't stand it. I'm getting out of here." He ran for the door and passed over a large metal floor register. He stopped and went back and waved his hand over the register and felt the heat blasting up. He pointed at Tony. *"You dirty creep you started a fire in the furnace and are trying to run us out."*

The other players jumped up and put their hands over the register and stared at Tony. Tony backed away from them with his hands up. "Wait a minute, you guys, I don't know what you're talking about, honest!" Tony knew there was no way to convince them. He dashed for the front door and made it outside. The players chased him.

"Unit 4, Bush and Erie, men in undershorts running after another guy in undershorts. Step it up, it sounds serious."

CHAPTER 16
THE PROPOSITION

Joe Martin was different from the other young men in the neighborhood. For one thing his family was rich. He never worked a day in his life. He had the best clothes and the latest model car. A braggart who believed he was a ladies' man. Everyone knew the only reason girls went out with him was to ride in his nice cars. Joe used to go to Murphy's Pool Hall and boast of all the pretty women he took out. The guys didn't pay any attention to him.

Joe's mother bought him a brand-new black Lincoln convertible. She told him to come outside to see the surprise she had for him. He walked out the door, looked at the car, showed no expression and got inside. His mother waited for him to say thank you, but he drove off.

He immediately went to Murphy's Pool Hall. As luck would have it there was a parking spot right in front. He pulled in and turned off the ignition. He sat behind the steering wheel and waited for someone to compliment his new car. As usual, no one paid any attention. He got out and slammed the door.

Hank Rapp was shooting pool and looked outside and saw Joe coming. "Everybody put on your hip boots, here comes lover-boy Martin. The bullshit is about to fly."

Joe entered the pool hall and slammed the door. No one looked up. They knew he did this to get attention. He walked to where Hank was playing and leaned on the table, flashing his large diamond ring. Hank shouted. "Get your damn hand off the table, I'm going to shoot!"

Joe slowly removed his hand then breathed on his ring and rubbed it on his shirt. "This ring cost seven hundred bucks."

Hank yelled back. "Who cares, keep the damn thing off the table or I'll make you eat it."

Joe took out his comb and passed it through his hair. "I didn't come here to be insulted.

I was going to offer you guys a proposition. I'm going to throw a big party next week and invite everyone of you. I know you're hard up for money so I'll furnish all the food and booze."

The pool hall became quiet as a tomb. Everyone quit playing. They were leaning on their cue sticks staring at Joe. Hank Rapp squinted. "So what's the catch?"

"I'm taking out this rich, refined, good looking broad next Tuesday. We're going to take a moonlight cruise on the ship Canadiana. I want to impress her. The deal is, you guys get on top of the Bean Docks. When the boat passes, me and the broad will be standing by the railing. You guys wave and shout, 'Hi Joe.' I'll wave back and yell, 'Hi guys.' That's all you got to do and I'll throw the big party."

Hank looked over at Franny Odell. Franny shrugged his shoulders and nodded his head as did all the other guys. "Okay, Martin, you're on."

"Good, now listen. The ship leaves the downtown dock at seven in the evening. It should pass the Bean Docks at seven-thirty. Get there a little early."

Hank pointed his pool stick at Joe. "We'll be there. You better keep your part of the deal!"

Joe assured him he would. Everybody went back to shooting pool. Joe tried to corner a couple of the guys and brag about his new car. They kept playing and didn't look up. Joe left the pool hall with a disgusted look and again slammed the door.

Tuesday evening Joe had his new car cleaned and shining with the top down. He pulled up in front of his date's home. She came running. "Oh, where did you get that beautiful car?"

Joe nonchalantly said, "Ah, it's nothing. I got another one

home that's better than this one. Wait just a minute, I'll put the top up so the wind won't mess your pretty hair."

Rose, his date, looked in amazement as the roof went up. He watched her eyes and thought, *I got her where I want her. Wait till the guys yell my name. That will put the frosting on the cake.*

The large excursion ship sounded two loud blasts from its horn and got under way. Joe grabbed Rose's hand and in his rude way elbowed and wedged his way through the people to get to the railing. Some of the people gave him a dirty look, but he didn't care.

Joe looked at his watch, it was five after seven. In the distance he could see the Bean Docks. Everything was going perfect. He pointed to the shore. "Rose, you see that big red building up there? That's where I went to high school. I played football and I was the star of the team. Someday I'll let you read my scrapbook." He pointed to a cluster of houses. "That's my neighborhood. I got a lot of friends up there. They all love me, especially the girls." He continued pointing and bragging as the boat cruised down the river. When they got closer to the Bean Docks Joe squinted. No one was standing on top. He cursed under his breath.

Meanwhile on the back side of the Bean Docks stood fifteen young men without any clothes on. Hank Rapp stood in front of the naked bunch. His hands were cupped around his mouth. "Now listen you guys! When I count to three we all run and jump off the dock." They lined up shoulder to shoulder. Hank saw the top of the smoke stack passing the docks."

Okay you guys, One, Two, Three. Sounds of slapping bare feet striking the concrete filled the air as the nude bodies dashed to the front of the dock and leaped.

Joe quit bragging and kept looking up, mumbling to himself. Rose felt something was wrong. "Is everything all right, Joe?"

He started to answer, but stopped abruptly when naked bodies exploded in the air above him. Their arms were outstretched and they shouted as they rained down. "Hi, Joe Martin, you big bull-shitter."

Startled, Rose and the other people at the railing jumped back as the naked bodies cascaded in front of them and plunged into the river.

Joe raised his fist. "I'm going to kill everyone of you idiots."

Back on top the Bean Docks one guy didn't jump. It was Franny Odell, the practical joker. He quickly gathered everyone's clothes and ran to Murphy's Pool Hall.

* * *

Police radios blared. "Units Four, and Five. Go to the shore of the Maumee River by the Bean Docks. The captain of the Canadiana reports that a large group of naked men jumped off the docks into the river."

"Units Two, and Three, go to the area of Galena and Erie Streets! Were getting numerous calls of men streaking."

CHAPTER 17
QUICK RESTITUTION

With his attorney at his side, Leon Bates stood before the judge. The judge asked him why he broke into his girlfriend's home. "Your Honor, I didn't mean to cause her any harm. I just wanted to borrow some money from her. She wasn't home at the time. I thought I would take it and repay her later."

His girlfriend shouted. "That's a damn lie. You had three months to give me back my money and you ain't given me a damn cent."

The judge banged his gavel. "There will be no more outbursts in my courtroom, is that understood?" The girlfriend nodded.

The judge asked her what she wanted to do about this matter. "All I want is my money back. I don't care what you do with the bum."

Leon sighed and smiled. "Your Honor, I will give her back the money. I just need a little time."

The judge looked at him and shook his head. "You had three months and you didn't give her anything. By a little time, you mean a couple of hours?"

Leon looked to his attorney. The attorney whispered something to him then shrugged his shoulders. Leon turned back to the judge. "Yes, Your Honor, I can get the money in two hours."

The judge looked at his watch. "Okay, if you're not back in two hours there will be a warrant issued for your arrest. No plea bargaining. Is that understood, Mr. Bates? The charge will be burglary if you don't return. Understood, Mr. Bates?"

"Yes, Your Honor, I understand." Leon ran from the courthouse and hailed a cab. He gave the driver an address. After traveling for about a block, he shouted, "Don't turn around. I got a gun and I'll blow your damn head off. Throw your wallet and all your money to me in the back seat."

The cab driver, fearing for his life, pitched his wallet and some change to the back seat. Leon grabbed the billfold and yelled, "Stop the cab. I'm getting out. After I leave you keep driving straight. Don't look back."

The cab driver watched the guy getting away with his hard-earned money. He screamed, "You, son-of-bitch." He got brave and jumped out of his cab and chased the robber.

Leon ran into the courthouse. The driver followed. When he got inside there was a crowd of people standing in the hall. He couldn't see the robber. He shouted, "Did anyone see a guy with gray pants and a white tee shirt run in here?" A man pointed to a door that had Court Room One written on it. The cabbie jerked the door open and ran inside. He saw the robber counting money from a wallet. He shouted, "That guy robbed me. That's my wallet the bastard has in his hand." He rushed to the robber and punched him. Police officers grabbed the cab driver and pulled him off Leon. The judge jumped up, pounding his gavel. Order was restored. The wallet was taken to the judge and he examined it. He asked the cab driver his name. The cab driver answered and the judge handed back his wallet.

The judge pointed at Leon Bates. "You're being charged with burglary and also robbery. Officers, take him away."

After booking Leon, one officer laughed, "I wonder what Leon will do to pay his fines this time?"

CHAPTER 18
DON'T FETCH

The cold wind howled, ice formed on the windows of Jim's Tavern, blocking the view to the outside. One by one, guys from the neighborhood came in stomping snow from their shoes and complaining how cold it was. A fire crackled in the fireplace. A table was slid in front of it and a card game was under way. Hours passed and the beers continued to flow. Charlie Bouton walked to the bar and looked at the snacks behind it. He mumbled, "There's nothing but junk back there." He looked at the guys at the table. "Hey, what you say we go ice fishing? I sure could go for some fresh fried fish." No one said a word. "Did you guys hear me?"

One of the card players looked at him like he was nuts.. "Have you been outside lately? It's freezing."

Charlie hit Bill Shroader on his shoulder. "Come on, Bill, you like to fish. We'll go and catch a bunch of perch and come back here and fry them up. You know how good they taste when they're caught in cold water."

Bill must have been hungry. He nodded and told the bartender to change his order from beer to whiskey. Slowly the other guys started to drink straight whiskey. Seeing this, Charlie knew they were warming themselves up to go. He told the bartender to give him a few bottles of whiskey and he would replace them later. He held up the bottles. "Come on you guys this will keep us warm." The group had a few more double shots, then bundled up and got in their pickup trucks and headed for the river.

The trucks were parked and the guys huddled outside by

the bank, shivering and swigging the whiskey. Bill Shroader looked at the frozen river and shook his head. "Man, that ice is a foot thick. Does anyone have an auger to make a hole?" No one answered. He shrugged his shoulders and started walking to his truck. "We'll never make a hole in that ice without an auger. I'm going back to the tavern. I'm not freezing my fanny off for nothing."

Charlie Bouton yelled. "Hold it, Bill, I've got something better than an auger. I was blowing tree stumps and I got a couple sticks of dynamite in my truck. Hell, we won't even need fishing poles when it goes off. Those fish will fly out of the water." He walked to his truck to get the dynamite and the other guys passed the whiskey around again.

Charlie came back with a red stick of dynamite. A wick dangled from one end of it.

He walked onto the ice and the rest of the group followed. He got about a hundred yards from shore and yelled, "Where's a good spot you guys?"

They pointed straight ahead and someone yelled, "About twenty yards in front of you." Charlie bent over to shield the wind from a match he lit. He put the flame to the wick and it sputtered sparks. He cocked his arm and threw the stick of dynamite to where they pointed. Immediately a large dog that followed them on the ice dashed for the stick of dynamite and almost caught it on the first bounce. He slid around, grabbed the dynamite in his mouth with the wick smoking and spitting sparks.

Bill Shroader yelled. "That crazy dog got the dynamite."

Someone else screamed. "He's fetching it back to us!"

Charlie had the whiskey bottle to his mouth. When he saw the dog coming back to him with the dynamite, his eyes widened. He dropped the bottle. Whiskey dribbled out of his open mouth. He tried to run on the ice, slipping and sliding. Everyone was trying to distance them selves from the dog by running, falling and crawling. They shouted for the dog to drop it but he kept coming.

When Units four and five arrived at the scene they

observed numerous windows blown out of cottages. A man was standing in front of his home screaming and swearing. He was pointing at a large hole in the ice. "Officers, I saw it all. A bunch of damn drunks got out on that ice and lit a stick of dynamite and threw it. A dog ran and got it and tried to retrieve to them. They ran like a bunch of wild drunken fools falling and crawling with the dog chasing after them. There was a loud explosion. Water flew in every direction. They got in their trucks and drove off.

The officers walked out onto the ice and noticed all kinds of fishing poles and tackle boxes abandoned. There was no sign of the dog or the men.

CHAPTER 19
ROBBING, CUSSING AND PRAYING

The room was filled with police. Some were in uniforms, others dressed in civilian clothes. Captain Caryle stood in front holding a long pointer aiming it at a floor plan of a home. He pointed to different parts of the house. "This is the kitchen. They keep the drugs in the freezer, packed in food bags." He then pointed at the bathroom. "It's important we gain control of these two rooms as fast as possible. We all know that as soon as we knock down the front door one guy will run to the freezer, grab the drugs and start flushing them down the toilet." He pointed at two officers. "You two will go to the west side of the house where the bathroom is. When you hear me give the order to knock down the front door, you guys break the bathroom window and stick the fire extinguisher inside and fog the room. The flusher, with the drugs will think it's some type of gas and scare hell out of him. He won't go in. I want the uniformed officers to follow right behind the guys with the ram pipe. When they knock down the door, you people rush in and make everyone lie on the floor. I want one guy on the entering team to run through the house, open the back door and let our men in. Remember you don't do anything until you hear my command. Is that understood?"

Some officers nodded and others responded, "Yes, Sir."

"Men, I want this to go off without any problems. Everyone's got his assignment. Remember we keep this house surrounded, so no one gets away. Keep it quiet and conceal yourselves. Are there any questions?" No one spoke. "Remember, you don't do anything until you hear my order over the radio. Okay, let's get out there and take this crack house down."

The ram team grabbed the handles of the heavy pipe filled with concrete and carried it to a truck. The Four of them will run the heavy pipe full speed into the front door and blast it open.

Splinters of wood will fly in every direction. The sight and sound of the door smashing will momentarily freeze everyone inside in their tracks.

The officers arrived at the crack house area in trucks borrowed from local businesses who had their logos on the sides so as not to give away the raid. They exited in alleys and then walked to their assigned places. In a short time everyone was ready. The men had their radios turned low and held them close to their ears. The captain's voice, just above a whisper, came over the radio. "Okay, men, keep it quiet and stay out of sight. The next time I get on the air it will be full go."

Everyone stared at the house. It was three o'clock in the morning and very dark. The men were tense waiting for the order. Suddenly windows flew open and men jumped out. One of them shouted, "Get my ass out of here. That fool's crazy. Somebody's going to get killed."

The captain shouted over the radio. "Damn it. Who spooked them? What the hell is going on? Knock down the front door." Four men picked up the heavy pipe and ran full speed to the front door. Just as the ram was going to slam into it, the door opened. A guy was dressed in camouflage clothing, He had a rifle and a white pillow case in his hands. The ram caught him flush in the stomach, his rifle and sack went flying. His body folded over the front of the ram as he was driven back into the house. The entry team was surprised when they got inside. People were lying on their stomachs with their arms out stretched in front of them. The officers in the rear rushed in. People slowly got up from the floor. They started kicking the guy who rode in on the front of the ram. The officers quickly pulled them away.

An officer shouted, "Quiet down. Don't move. What's

going on in here?"

Someone screamed, "That crazy son-of-a-bitch robbed us. He's got our billfolds in that pillow case."

Officers searched the freezer but didn't find any drugs. They turned the pillow case upside down. Wallets, and drugs wrapped in freezer bags, dropped to the floor.

Twelve people were transported to the detective bureau by paddy wagons for questioning. I was assigned to interview them. I recognized a few faces that I had dealings with before. I told the uniformed officers to get the names and birth dates of all the men taken in and check for warrants. One by one I brought them into the interrogation room. Some of them were tough harden criminals. I asked one guy. "You and your friends are mean people who can handle yourselves. Why didn't you disarm that guy?"

"Man, I want to tell you about that fool. He came in the place dressed in all that camouflage and aiming that gun at everybody. He fired a shot in the ceiling and yelled for us to get on the floor. Then he robbed us, while cussing and screaming prayers at the same time. You know that sorry bastard has to be a damn nut to pray, rob and cuss at the same time. Man, I don't mess with crazy people when they got a gun."

I tried to talk to the robber. He just sat there speechless in his camouflaged clothing. I went back into the other room where the twelve guys were being held. An officer handed me a sheet of paper. Out of the twelve who were brought in, eight had warrants. I called out their names and advised them they were under arrest. One of them jumped up. "Ain't this a bitch? The fool robs me and I go to jail."

I quickly informed him that he was being arrested for an outstanding warrant. He asked what the warrant was for? I told him bastardy. He said what is that? I said laying pipe without a license. He understood that.

All the men arrested asked if they could ride to jail with the guy who robbed them.

I told them, "Request denied.

CHAPTER 20
DEMENTED MAN IN THE FOUNTAIN

It was Harry's big day. The long wait was over. His interview for a promotion was set for this morning before the Board Of Directors. The step up from middle management too executive overwhelmed him. He took a deep breath. "Everything about me has to be perfect."

He dressed carefully and slowly. He took the new expensive silk suit off the hanger so not to wrinkle it. His shirt, tie, even his underwear and socks had been placed carefully on the bedroom chair the night before. After he had his pants on, he rubbed his socks over his highly polished shoes in case dust fell on them during the night.

He stood before the mirror examining every detail of his appearance. Straining his neck, he turned to make sure the back draped well. He did a little jig and shouted. "I'm one sharp guy. Bring them on. Just lemme' at 'em... I'm gonna' get that promotion because, *I am perfect!*"

The parking lot behind the Trion Building was full causing Harry to cuss under his breath. He squealed tires and parked a block away. Getting out of the car it felt like a blast furnace. He mumbled, "Jeez, It's like a day in Hell." He hoped the sweat wouldn't ruin his new gray suit before his interview.

As he approached the fountain in front of the Trion Building, he noticed a group of young boys playing in the water. Generally this wasn't allowed but today was a scorcher. He didn't pay them any attention. He was thinking of the interview. The kids squealed and danced under streams of cool water cascading over their bare backs.

As Harry approached, he turned to steal a quick glance at himself at every store window he passed. "Yes, indeedy', I sure look good." At the window just before the Trion Building, he pulled out a comb and passed it through his hair, then straightened his tie once more. He smiled at himself, "Yessirree, those big shots can't help but think they've gotta' winner here."

Harry didn't go unnoticed by the boys splashing and jumping around in the stone fountain. One of them yelled, "Hey, you guys, look at that goof over there smiling to himself. He looks like he's got a coat hanger stuck in his mouth the way he's grinning. Let's splash his ass."

Harry's mind was focused on the interview and the promotion. He didn't notice the boys on their hands and knees crawling like alligators closer to the side of the fountain where he would pass. One of them sprung up and yelled. "Give it to him." The other boys exploded up splashing Harry.

This caught Harry by surprise. His mouth opened, water dripped from his head and his silk suit. Another wave hit him before he could react. He was drenched. Realizing what had happened, he made two fists and screamed strange choking sounds. The boys laughed and kept splashing.

"You rotten little bastards, I'll kill you." They quit splashing and ran to the far side of the fountain. Harry dove into the fountain trying to get his hands on them. The boys knew it wasn't time to stick around. This guy with the crazed look and screaming caused them to jump out of the fountain. Naked except for their underwear, they ran for safety. Their bare feet slapping on the pavement. They didn't look back. Harry continued to scream, cuss and threaten as he stomped around in the fountain flailing the air with his fists.

The police dispatcher's voice crackled over the radio. "Unit one and Three. Go to the front of the Trion Building. We're getting numerous calls concerning a demented man fully clothed, in the middle of the fountain screaming."

CHAPTER 21
TWO GHOSTS SNATCHED MY RIBS

Just outside Detroit. Michigan two fourteen-year old boys were staring at the large railroad yard. Fascinated by the many tracks and trains it was only a short time and they were climbing one of the boxcars. They ran on the wire mesh walk on top and jumped from one boxcar to another. Jim's feet landed on a large metal one. He shouted,

"Hey, Doug, look at all the hatches on top of this one. I wonder what's inside." He grabbed a large handle and turned it. He pulled the hatch cover slightly open but couldn't get it open all the way.

"Doug, give me a hand. This is heavy."

Doug, grabbed the handle and both of them strained, grunted and finally pulled the cover open. Jim, dropped to his knees and leaned in. "Man, you ought to see all the white stuff in here. Put your head down there and take a look."

Doug moved forward and was starting to lean over when he tripped on a metal object protruding from the roof of the boxcar. He fell onto Jim's back and both dropped head first into the boxcar. They were immediately engulfed by the white powder.

"Doug, where you at? What is this stuff?" He heard spitting sounds.

"I'm over here. It tastes like flour. We got to get out of here."

They crawled to the shaft of light coming from the open hatch. Doug, raised his arm and grabbed the heavy hatch cover and started to pull himself up when the hatch cover slammed shut. The inside of the boxcar went dark. He raised his hand to the metal door and pushed. "Jim, we're in a mess. It's locked." They both pushed at the hatch cover but it wouldn't budge. They pounded their fists on the thick metal. It only made muffled thumping noises. They shouted until they got hoarse but the sound would not penetrate the thick metal enclosure.

"Doug, we're in a jam. We're locked in here. We got to settle down and figure this out."

"Yeah, I know what you mean. Now I know how those fish filets felt like when my mother put them in a bag of flour and shook, before frying them."

"Hey, this ain't funny. We got to get out of here. We're in serious trouble."

The boys didn't say anymore. The inside of the boxcar became silent. Hours passed then a loud bang followed by a sudden jerk that shook the boxcar.

"Jim, what's that? I think we're moving."

"I know we're moving I can feel it. Oh, man, I wonder where we're going. I hope it's not far."

The squealing of the metal wheels on the tracks made talking impossible. The boys got themselves as comfortable as they could. Hours passed, then the train slowed down. A loud screeching sound and it stopped.

"Doug, we're not moving. I wonder where we're at?"

"I don't know but it sure is nice having it quiet."

"Jim, did you hear that? It sounds like someone is walking on top." The boys strained their ears as the faint sound of footsteps got louder.

"Doug, I bet it's the railroad police. They came to arrest us. Let's crawl under that hatch and when they open it we'll jump out and run as fast as we can. Don't stop for anything."

"Don't worry, I don't want to get caught either. The boys got in position under the hatch.

Two men above put down their clip boards and measuring instruments and unlocked the hatch. They both grabbed the heavy door. The boys heard the click of the door being unlocked. They bent their knees. The hatch door came open and light exploded in. The boys sprung out. The startled railroad men let out a scream and jumped backwards away from the open hatch.

Jim and Doug scrambled down the metal ladder on the side of the boxcar. They jumped over numerous tracks and ran into an alley. Halfway through they stopped and looked back. No one was following. Doug bent over with his hands on his knees. Jim was leaning against a garage. Both of them were breathing hard.

After they rested a few minutes, Doug looked at Jim and began to laugh. He was laughing so hard he had to sit and hold his stomach.

"What's so funny?"

"Man, look at you. The only thing that ain't white is your eyeballs and mouth. Your hair is pure white, and so is your clothes."

"Well, look at you, you're the same way. How we going to get this stuff off?"

They jumped up and down slapping at their clothes. Two white clouds erupted around them.

Doug shouted as he bounced up and down. "You look like a big powder puff. I don't think this stuff will ever come off."

"I'm not worried about that. I'd like to know where we're at. I sure am hungry. Do you have any money?"

"No, I'm broke. Lets keep walking, maybe we'll see a sign."

They continued through the alley. Doug stopped abruptly and started sniffing. "Smell that, Jim? Someone is barbecuing."

"Yeah, it smells good. I see smoke coming from that backyard. Let's check it out."

The boys slid their backs along a garage and peeked into the yard A man was cooking two large slabs of meat and brushing brown liquid from a pan on them. The boy's mouths watered as they watched him. The man looked into the pan and noticed it was empty. He went into his home to get more sauce.

The boys saw their chance. They jumped the fence and ran to the grill. Both grabbed a slab of meat.

Jim shouted, "Man this meat is hot, it's burning my hands."

"Just keep throwing it up in the air and catching it, it will cool off and you'll be able to handle it."

The man heard noises coming from his back yard. He quickly opened the door and ran out. He stopped immediately when he saw these white things dancing and throwing his meat in the air. He ran back in the house and grabbed the phone. "Listen, police. You're not going to believe this."

"Unit Eleven, this is the dispatcher. Go to five-twelve Avondale. A man reports there are two strange things in his back yard."

Unit Eleven pulled up in front of five twelve Avondale. A man ran out of the house waving his arms. He had a frightened look. He shouted, "Officers two ghosts done snatched my ribs. I was cooking in the back yard and they grabbed the ribs right off the grill. They were tossing my ribs up and dancing. Man, don't say I'm crazy, because I know what I saw."

CHAPTER 22
CAT-A-PULT

An elderly lady yelled and waved to a scout car passing by. The officer on the passenger side saw her and shouted to his partner. "Bill, turn around, that woman wants us." Bill made a quick U-turn and drove back to her.

"Officers, can you help? My cat climbed to the top of that tree and can't get down."

The young officer nodded. "Sure." He reached for the mike in the cradle.

His partner knew what he was going to do. "That won't be necessary, Pat. No need bothering the fire department. I'm sure we can handle it."

"But, Bill, those limbs are thin where that cat is. We'll never be able to climb out on them."

"Who said anything about climbing? I once had the same situation and we got the animal down all right." Pat stared at him in disbelief. Bill got out of the car and walked to the backyard of the home. He untied a clothesline from the poles and wrapped it from his hand to his elbow. He picked up a loose brick from under a garbage can. Pat, the other officer and the old lady watched Bill as he tied the brick to one end of the clothesline.

The old lady looked concerned. "You're not going to hit my cat with that brick are you?"

"No ma'am. Everything is going to be all right. We'll have him down in a minute."

They walked to the front yard. Bill pointed to a spot under the tree. "Pat, stand there. I'm going to throw this brick over that thick part of the limb where the cat is. When the brick comes down you take it and I'll take this side. We'll pull the rope until it bends the branch down enough so we can grab the cat."

Bill threw the brick with the rope over the branch. Everything was going as planned. Both officers pulled down on the rope until the branch started to bend. The older officer shouted. "Pat, this is the tough part. We really have to pull hard to get it bent low enough for us to reach the cat. Give it all you got."

Both officers strained as they reached one hand over the other bringing the branch closer to the ground. The branch looked like an inverted letter "C" and was now low enough to grab the cat. Pat reached for it when a loud pop sound pierced through the neighborhood. The clothesline snapped, the limb recoiled and the cat catapulted, turning somersaults high in the air. It flew about sixty feet and landed feet first on the roof of a neighbor's home.

The little old lady had her hands drawn up in fists. "I oughta' kick your asses."

Officer Pat stood next to the house looking up at the cat. It hissed, back hunched up, eyes glared and fur bristled. Pat shouted to his partner. "Bill, what do we do now?"

"Now you call the fire department. That cat is wild. After all, it's their job."

CHAPTER 23
GO AHEAD AND SHOOT

Jim and Larry were in the sporting goods store buying supplies for a bear hunting trip out west. The salesman asked if they ever hunted bear before. Both men shook their heads. "Well, I'll give you some good advice. You better have a dependable sidearm for backup."

Larry stared at him. "What do you mean, a dependable sidearm?"

"Well, you're hunting with a bow. If you don't hit a vital spot that bear will turn and attack. They can run fast and if he charges, you won't be able to get another arrow off. Most guys carry a sidearm."

Jim nodded. "I think he's right. I heard of a guy who shot a bear in the ass with an arrow. The damn thing got mad and caught the guy and mauled him. He was lucky another hunter was close by and shot the bear."

The two men talked it over and Larry spoke up again. "Where do you have your hand guns?"

The salesman nodded. "Over there. Follow me."

The two hunters looked at the large selection of revolvers and automatics. Larry asked, "What do you recommend?"

"Well, if it was up to me, I'd buy a powerful revolver. An automatic sometimes jams. If a big bear is coming after me, I want something that will drop him with no chance of the gun jamming." He reached into the display case and pulled out a blue steel revolver. "Now, this is a three-fifty-seven magnum. If you shoot a bear with it, I can assure you it will stop him in his tracks."

Larry and Jim handled the gun and examined every fine feature. Both agreed they should each get one. Larry said, "Give us the guns and six boxes of bullets."

The clerk reached behind and got the bullets off a shelf and put them on the counter.

"These are hot loads. They're more powerful than the normal bullet. I'm sure they'll do the job if the occasion arises." The men paid for their purchases and left.

"Come on, Jim, we got one more place to go."

"What do you mean one more place to go?"

"Well, we got to practice. We'll go to the liquor store and pick up a few bottles of wine and go to Old Ed's place down by the river. I'm sure he'll let us shoot if he sees the wine."

"Hey, you're right. That old drunk would let us do anything for a drink."

A couple days later they drove down an unpaved dusty road. When they came to a dilapidated house surrounded by high weeds, Jim jammed on the brakes. The car slid sideways into the front yard. A dusty cloud that had followed, engulfed it. Larry and Jim jumped out of the car and waved the dust away from their faces. The front door flew open. A bearded older man in coveralls stained with tobacco juice and drained oil ran to them with his fists in the air. "What the hell is the matter with you two jerks?"

Larry and Jim quickly grabbed the bottles of wine and held them up. "We'd like to talk with you, Ed."

Old Ed's mean expression melted and his eyes widened as he stared at the bottles. "What you want to talk about? I'm all ears."

Jim handed him a bottle. "Well, we'd like to do some target practice down by the river. Old Ed didn't reply. He kept looking at the remaining bottles the men were holding.

Jim and Larry handed him the wine.

"Sure, you can shoot anytime, just as long as you bring me a taste. Come on, I'll show you where to go." He led them down a path littered with beer cans and wine bottles. The weeds on both sides were taller then the men. They finally came to a clearing by a road near the river.

Larry and Jim started picking up beer cans for targets when Larry saw an old car.

"Hey, Ed, is it okay if we shoot that abandoned car?"

Ed lowered the wine bottle from his mouth. "Yeah, go ahead and shoot it."

Larry and Jim dropped to one knee, opened the cylinders to their revolvers and loaded them with the powerful bullets. Larry was first to stand. He took aim at the windshield. A loud explosion and the windshield shattered sending pieces of glass in every direction. The projectile blew out the windshield then traveled through the seats and exploded the rear window. "Man, this is a powerful gun. Be careful, it kicks like a mule."

Jim aimed at a headlight. A loud bang and the glass disintegrated. Where once there was a light, now was a large hole. Jim laughed. "Man, these guns are something. The bullets go through metal like it's paper." The two men positioned themselves so they were facing the side of the car. They shot out all the windows. Jim looked at Larry. "Hey, we need a smaller target. You see that little chrome disk where you unlock the door? Let's see if we can hit it." They took turns firing at it. In no time there was a gaping cavity. They walked to the car to examine it.

Larry pointed inside the car. "Damn, look in there. Those bullets either went through the door and exited the other side, or they ricocheted inside and tore up the dashboard. They not only put holes in the car, they chewed hell out of everything in their way." The two, went to the back of the car and shot up the trunk. There wasn't a visible part on that car that didn't have bullet holes in it.

"Hey, Larry, we're out of ammo. I can't believe we shot three hundred rounds." They picked up the empty brass casings and stared at the car. Jim shook his head. "That salesman at the sports store was right. These guns are powerful. That car looks like a flight of fighter planes strafed it." He looked over at Old Ed who had the gallon bottle of wine to his mouth. "Hey, Ed, How long has that car been here?"

Old Ed lowered the bottle. He looked at the car. "I don't know, I never saw it before today. It probably belongs to a guy fishing down there."

"What?"

When the officer responded to the call he got out of his car. A man was pointing and cussing at a bullet-ridden car. The officer's eyes widened. "I'd say, someone don't like you."

CHAPTER 24
ALL IN A DAYS WORK

After interviewing a robbery victim my partner and I were leaving the hospital driveway when the dispatcher called another car. "Unit 12, we have a lady on the phone yelling for help at 2025 Adams Street. Step it up because we can't determine what's going on."

I looked at my partner. "We're only a couple of blocks away, want to jump that call?"

He nodded, "Yeah."

"Dispatcher, this is Unit 9, we're close to that address. Do you want us to take it?"

"Unit 9, assist Unit 12. We don't know what's going on at that address. A woman is screaming in the phone and not making any sense."

We were forced back into the seat as Andy accelerated the car. A couple of turns on side streets and we were on Adams Street. In front of us a block away was Unit 12. Its red rotating lights cut circular streaks into the misty night. A bright white beam from its spotlight searched the buildings for an address. The brake lights went on and both officers ran from the car. Andy brought our car to a stop and we rushed after the officers.

We flung the door open to a rundown apartment house. A large stairway was ahead of us. We took the steps two at a time. The second floor was almost dark. A lonesome light bulb hanging on a frayed cord strained to shed some light. Instead of burning white it was a faded yellow due to the accumulated dust on it. The dark colored wallpaper seemed to suck in what little light it was emitting. The doors to the apartments were painted dark brown making a depressing contrast..

From the far end of this catacomb came a barrage of cussing. The four of us lit our flash lights and aimed the beams at the voice. A frail little lady about eighty years old appeared. A petticoat draped over her small body. Nylon socks were rolled down to her worn slippers. Her thin arms shielded her eyes from our bright lights.

"Get those god damn lights out of my eyes, you stupid bastards." We lowered the lights and approached her, playing the lights to the left and right of her. I couldn't believe that language was coming from this little old woman. There must be a lumberjack or a Drill Sergeant with her. To my surprise she was alone.

An officer from the other crew asked. "Ma'am did you call the police?"

"Your damn right I called. It took me three months to save up enough money to buy one of your police radios and the no good piece of junk won't work."

The officer shook his head. "Wait a minute lady, we don't sell those radios. We're only heard on them. We just answer calls. The police department has nothing to do with selling them."

I could tell by her expression she was hard of hearing. Nothing the officer said got through to her. He looked at his partner who was also confused. He turned to her and again tried to explain. She held the transistor in front of her and told the officer where he could stick it.

Andy smiled and put out his hand. "Let me see it, please." She gave it to him and Andy's large hand engulfed it. He squinted in the dim light as he tried to examined it. I aimed my flash light at the radio so he could see it better.

Seeing this the old lady shouted a barrage of filthy words against the light condition.

"That cheap sonabitchin landlord should have rented to blind people. Then he could turn off all the damn lights in this dump." She pointed to an open door. "Come on, let's get the hell out of here and go to my place."

We went into her meager apartment. Andy hooked his foot under a chair and pulled it away from the kitchen table. He laid the little transistor on the table, sat down and popped the back off it. She leaned over his shoulder and watched everything he did. A cigarette dangled from the corner of her mouth. Her head bobbed back and forth trying to dodge the swirl of smoke from going into her eyes. Andy wasn't aware she was standing over him due to his concentration with the inner workings of the small radio. All at once, he looked up. "She had the batteries in wrong."

He rearranged the batteries and snapped the back on. Almost immediately the dispatcher's voice came over the radio. "Unit 13, go to 707 North Erie Street. Burglary in progress." The old lady's eyes widened. She grabbed Andy around the neck and hugged him.

"Now, that's what I want to hear. That's why I bought the damn thing."

Andy got up and handed her the radio. She grabbed it and put it next to her ear and smiled at Andy. "You work for a hell of a company. They really back up their products. They meant what they said in the guarantee. Can you imagine, I called and in three minutes four repairmen showed up and no charge. Hell, one time I bought a T.V. and it took three weeks for a repairman to come. The damn thing never was right after that idiot worked on it. I also had to pay for a service call. I'm going to tell all my friends, what a nice outfit you are."

Andy threw up his hands and stuttered. "No, no, ma'am, you don't need to do that."

She walked us to the steps. On the way down one of the officers called the dispatcher.

"This is Units 12 and 9, we're both in service at 2025 Adams Street."

Like other calls people gathered in front of the building. Someone shouted, "What happened?"

We gave the usual answer. "Everything is all right. Lets

break it up."

We were getting in our cars when a loud shrill voice came from a second story window. The old lady was hanging half way out with the radio in her hand.

"Hey you guys, I just heard my address on the police radio. What does that mean?"

The younger officer from Unit 12, looked up. "Ma'am it means----."

The older officer grabbed him by the arm. "Come on, we spent too much time here already." We got into our cruisers, the red lights were turned off, and we rambled into the darkness ready for the next call.

The little old lady pulled herself back inside and closed the window. The people in front walked away mumbling.

This call will not make the news media, but it's one of the many things that happens in a days work of a police officer.

CHAPTER 25
YEEEOW

Three teenage boys huddled in a thicket on the school playground. It was dark and they were making plans to burglarize the school. Willie, the oldest and the leader instructed the other two. "Now listen, first we break a window. Then we hide to see if anyone hears the noise. If no one comes out of their homes, we run to the broken window and climb inside. No lights and don't make any noise. You guys got it straight?"

Neither boy said anything. They just nodded. Willie pushed them. "Can't you guys talk? What's the matter, you scared?"

Leroy blurted out. "Naw, man, we're not scared. Let's get it on."

"All right then. James, go down that alley and find me a brick. Don't let anyone see you." James crawled out of the bushes and faded into the darkness. In a short time he reappeared in front of the thicket. Willie whispered, "Man, just don't stand there. Get in here with us, you damn fool." James parted the bushes and sat next to Willie. He handed him the brick. Willie grabbed it and shouted. "You dummy, I said a brick. Not a half one."

"Man, what's the difference, a full brick, or a half brick? It's dark in that alley and that's all I could find."

Willie got mad. "Dummy, a full brick will break out more glass then a half brick. Now, do you get it?"

"Well, I ain't going back in that alley. If you want to break twice as much glass throw the damn half brick two times through the window."

Willie was about to explode. "I got a better idea. I'll hit you twice with that half brick. Then I'll hit you once with a full brick and you tell me which hurts more."

There was no more conversation about bricks. Willie, again gave orders. "You guys stay here." He parted the branches, hunched over and ran toward the school with the half brick in his hand. He took aim at a first story window and slung the brick. The sound of glass breaking echoed through the neighborhood. He turned, ran and dove back into the bushes.

Ten minutes passed. Willie's head popped up from the bushes. He looked around and no one came out of their homes. "Okay you guys follow me. They bent over and ran for the broken window. Willie pulled the remaining jagged pieces from the window frame and climbed into the dark school. James and Leroy were right behind.

Willie again warned about lights and noise. "If you turn on any lights the cops will see it from the outside. Do you understand?"

"Yeah, we hear you."

Willie went to the teacher's desk. The other two opened the students desks. James asked, "How do we know what is good to steal if we can't see it?"

Willie yelled. "You feel for it, you idiot. If it feels good, take it."

"Man, I don't know how to feel. I'm going to light a match so I can see what's good."

"If you light a damn match I'll show you how it feels to have my fist go upside your damn head. You hear me, James?"

James got the message, no matches were lit. They took things from this classroom and went back into the hall. The sound of them walking and scratching their finger nails on the metal lockers echoed throughout the deserted school. Willie kept warning them to be quiet.

They entered other classrooms rifling the desks. Not much

of value was found. At the end of the hall there was a different type door. Willie tried to open it but it was locked. "Hot damn, this is the one. This door is locked. It must be the room where they keep all the good stuff." He pulled off his shoe and slammed it into the small window shattering the glass. He reached through the broken window and unlocked the door.

They rushed in and couldn't wait to get to the valuable stuff. It was much darker and warmer than the other rooms. Willie as before went directly to the teacher's desk. The other two separated and went to the back. In their haste they bumped into objects sending them crashing to the floor.

Willie, shouted, "Man, if you fools get me caught making that noise I'll beat you into tomorrow."

Leroy thought he made a real find when his hands bumped into some large boxes on a shelf. "James, get over here. I think the good stuff is in these boxes."

"Where you at, Leroy? I can't see a thing. Keep talking so I can find you."

Leroy kept saying, "Over here, over here." James kept his arms outstretched and feeling his way to him.

Leroy grabbed James's hand and put it on one of the large boxes. James quickly felt the box. It was made of wood and chicken wire. His hand moved across the top and made contact with a metal latch. It clicked when he pushed a small lever. He felt the other side and did the same with that latch. He pushed on the upper part of the box. The top came loose and crashed to the floor.

Another warning from the front of the room. "One more noise, dummy and I'm coming back there. You understand?"

James didn't answer, he was busy probing his hand inside the box. He was disappointed at first since he sensed the box was empty. He stood on his tiptoes and reached deeper. His hand hit something. He grasped it. It was tubular in shape. He couldn't get his hand around it so he grabbed with both hands. It felt like a fire hose with water running through it. He squeezed and it started to move. It became hard and muscles began to expand and pull together. Feeling this, he knew that whatever he had in his hands was alive. He screamed, "Yeeeow, get my ass out of here." He bulldozed through desks and chairs.

Leroy, yelled. "What's the matter, James?" James didn't answer. Leroy knew something was really wrong for James to act this way. He had no choice but to light a match. The flickering flame lit a horrifying sight. A large boa constrictor, its eyes shining from the light slithered out of an overturned cage on the floor. "Aw shit, man," He jumped on top of a desk and jumped to another one.

Willie heard all the commotion. "Man, I had enough of you guys." He clenched his fist and ran to the back. "I told you fools not to light a match. Now I'm going to bust your heads."

He stopped abruptly when he heard James's terrifying scream. "Snake, big snake."

"Say what? What you saying about a snake?"

Leroy's voice full of panic. "James, let a big snake out and it's crawling on the floor."

All three boys were now jumping from one desk top to another, each with a lit match in their hand. Back in the hallway they distanced themselves from the room as fast as they could. They crashed into the walls in their hasty retreat, losing all their loot. After much confusion, screaming and cussing they found the room with the broken window. Each tried to get out first. Willie grabbed James and Leroy by the back of their pants and flung them away from the window. He climbed out and the other two were right behind him.

Willie dove into the bushes. As soon as James crawled in he grabbed him by the front of his shirt and pushed his fist in James face. "I'm going to knock every tooth out of your hollow head." He started to carry out the threat but James was shaking so bad Willie turned him loose. The three ran home and nothing more was said about the break-in, or the snake.

The next day I was assigned the case. I went to the school and talked with the principal. He immediately directed me to the science room. This room was in disarray. The principal smiled and pointed to a wooden cage. "One of the burglars must of knocked over that cage and the snake got loose. I believe the snake scared them off. The science teacher found the snake in the hallway and put him back."

I noticed there were prints from the soles of shoes on top of the desks. One print was unique. There was a star and a gouge mark that must of been made when the subject who was wearing this shoe stepped on something sharp. I took a picture of this print. Later I went to a shoe store and showed the picture to a salesman. He showed me a tennis shoe by the name of Converse. I looked at the sole and there was a star in the middle of it.

Later when I went to the high schools in the area and talked to suspects on other investigations I always looked at the shoes they were wearing. Eventually I saw one of the suspects wearing Converse tennis shoes. I asked him to raise his feet so I could see the soles of his shoes. I saw the star and the gouge mark.

I looked him in the eye and said, "Willie, did you break into that grade school so you could pet that snake?"

His eyes got wide. "Man, are you out of your mind?" He then gave me a complete account of the incident.

I went back to the grade school and told the principal the case was solved. I gave him some good advice. "Let the snake roam the halls at night. I'm sure there wouldn't be anymore break-ins."

CHAPTER 26
HE'S IMPORTANT

There was only one thing left to do for the police charity show; pick up the performers at the Detroit Metro Airport for the Roy Radin show and I was designated to get them. There was Tiny Tim, Georgie Jessel, Frank Fontaine (Crazy Gugenheimer), Frank Gorsham, and Donald O'Connor. The plane arrived at three in the afternoon and the show was at eight that evening at the Masonic Hall in Toledo.

I went into the airport and held my sign up that read Roy Radin show. People streamed past me, then I heard this loud deep voice, shout. "Hey, you with the sign." I looked and there was Georgie Jessel waving his hand. I walked to him and introduced myself and we waited for the other four. People stopped and stared as a crowd gather. Some people came forward with pencils and paper in their hands asking for autographs. Georgie Jessel stood on his tiptoes so he could see over the crowd and shouted to the other performers. "Get your ass in gear. We got to get the hell outta here." He grabbed my arm. "Take us to the car or we're going to have a riot.

I ran and they followed. I opened the van doors and they threw their luggage inside and grabbed seats. The crowd followed and were yelling the actors' names. The stars waved and smiled. Georgie Jessel's deep voice caused vibrations. "Give it the gas. Get us the hell outta here." I managed to steer in and out of the crowd without hitting anyone. It was quiet for about ten minutes, then the distinctive voice of Jessel sounded again. "Can you take us to a nice quiet place where we can get a drink and something to eat without a lot of bullshit from people bothering us?"

"Yeah, I know a place. I belong to the V.F.W and it's private. People there will leave you alone." Everyone agreed that would be the perfect place to spend the next couple of hours before the show.

I put my membership card in the slot, heard a dull ring, then a click. We entered and sat at the bar. Bernie the bartender, a friend of mine, walked up behind the bar. "What do you and your friends waa----?" He stopped talking and squinted at the performers. He leaned over and looked directly in my eyes. "Bob, what the hell is going on? I know who those guys are. What are they doing in here?"

I started to explain, when Georgie Jessel, who was sitting next to me, placed his hand on my wrist and said. "Bob, here, is a good friend of ours. Every year we come to Toledo and visit him. He's a great guy."

Bernie's eyes widened. Frank Gorsham sided in. "Hasn't Bob, told you of his past. You ought to feel privileged to have him as a member. He looked at the other three. "Ain't that right you guys?" They nodded. He looked at me. "Bob, you old devil, you. You were always too modest."

I just sat there at a lost for words. It felt like everyone in the place was staring at me and whispering. The stars enjoyed the V.F.W. They ate their meals and had a few drinks without anyone disturbing them.

We stayed about two hours when Georgie Jessel's deep voice growled extra loud. "Well, Bob, it's time to pick up Bing and Bob Hope. After all they are looking forward to seeing you." I slowly got up and walked to the door dumbfounded. All my friends made a special effort to say goodbye.

On the way to the Masonic Hall the four of them laughed and joked about how the people in the V.F.W looked when Georgie Jessel told them they were visiting me. He said. "Bob, you are now the most popular guy in the club. You ought to run for one of the offices."

I forced a smile. "I don't know whether to be mad or glad."

I drove them to the hall and they put on a wonderful show. Afterwards, I drove them back to Detroit Metro. Before getting out of the van they shook my hand and said. "We're coming back to Toledo next year to visit." We all laughed. Their plane took off into the darkness and I never saw them again.

I went in the V.F.W numerous times after that. Almost every time Bernie and other members would question me about my past and how I knew those guys. Every time I started to tell them the true story I could feel Georgie Jessel's hand on my wrist and I would go silent. I guess, I like being an important person.

CHAPTER 27
GET THAT COP

While stopped for the red light on the way to the police station, I studied the people going in and out of the numerous bars located along this section of the city, known as skid row. I thought, it won't be long and I'd be making acquaintances with some of them for various reasons. This is my district, Unit 4, where I work as a police officer on a paddy wagon better known as the Black Mariah Our motto was, "You call, we haul."

This looked like a good night for business. The weather was warm and it was Saturday night. Groups of people were moving aimlessly on the sidewalks, going in and out of the brightly lit cafes like swarms of moths attracted by the lights. Unlike the moths, these people were all different and had their own reasons for being on skid row.

When the light turned green I continued to the station. After roll call, my partner Frank and I checked out the Mariah. Frank jumped behind the steering wheel. He knew it was going to be a busy night and the best place was to be the driver. The other officer had to ride in back with the people who have been arrested. Most of them were drunk and take out their frustrations on that officer.

Frank looked at me. "How does it look on the corners (skid row)?"

"Why you ask me a question like that? You know it's going to be crazy. That's why you jumped into the driver's seat. I'm telling you, Frank, it's crowded, there's enough characters down there to write a comic strip."

We were patrolling when the dispatcher called our number. "Unit Four, In the alley behind the Highway Bar a beat officer has a man down." We okayed the call.

When we entered the mouth of the alley, we saw the officer waving his flashlight.

Frank drove slowly with the bright lights on since this alley was known for drunks sleeping in it. The beat officer was standing over a man on the ground struggling to get to his feet. The guy smelled of stale wine and made no sense when he tried to talk. We determined he couldn't take care of himself, so we'd give him a ride to jail in the Black Maria.

Frank, the beat officer and I lifted him into the paddy wagon and propped him in the corner so he wouldn't fall. I got in with him. I looked him over. He must be six foot two, and weighed about two hundred and fifty pounds. His head rocked back and forth and he fell asleep. I was glad. They don't fight when they're sleeping. Everything was going nice and peaceful but as luck would have it we hit a deep pothole. One eye of the drunk popped open and was exploring his new surroundings. It now was staring at me. His other eye exploded open. I thought, here we go. Is he going to be a shouter or a fighter? I don't mind the shouter. Words don't hurt. A fighter can make it rough on my body and uniform.

The guy not only had his eyes working. His mouth was in gear, "I haven't done anything wrong, you son-of-a-bitch. Bet you feel good taking me to jail. You'll probably make sergeant for arresting me." I just let him sound off. They taught us about situations like this. Although, I thought, buddy I have some good names for you, too, but I kept quiet. Whatever he had been drinking over took him again. His chin dropped to his chest and he fell asleep. He started to gurgle. The stale wine was about to come up. I didn't want to get sprayed. I grabbed the neck of his sweat shirt and lifted it over his mouth. The wine gushed up and went inside his shirt. Not a drop got on me or the Maria.

At the jail we took him out of the wagon the same way he went in. Once we got him into a cell, we put him on a cot to sleep it off. He woke up, "I'm going to plead not guilty and I'm going to have your jobs."

Frank, laughed. "Mister. You'll have to stand in line. Good night."

Another call came in. "Large bar fight, Green Lantern Night Club." This sounded like a good one since three crews were answering it. When we pulled up in front, the huge window was completely broken out. Bodies, bottles, and chairs were flying in all directions. It reminded me of a pirate movie with men battling from one ship to another. There were no bystanders. Everyone was involved in this brawl. We waded in, ducking breaking glass and flying chairs. It took fifteen minutes to restore order. Five men were taken to the hospital, six were arrested and stuffed into the Maria. I rode on the outside on a step in the back holding onto the bar above the door.

Two more calls and both were up to par, loud and abusive. At four-thirty in the morning the tension had built to its peak. Frank rubbed his eyes. "It looks like it's going to slow down." He no sooner said it when we got another call to pick up a woman for intoxication. The arresting officers put her in the back of our wagon. I got in and sat down. She immediately started cussing and calling me every dirty name she knew. I glanced at her and shook my head. I was numb from the other calls and didn't care what she said.

When we got her to the women's jail, the matrons took her to a private room to search her to see if she had any weapons or drugs concealed on her person. One of the matrons screamed. "You no good rotten pervert." Frank and I rushed into the room. The matrons glared at us. It seems we didn't have a woman but a man dressed up like one. The matrons gave us a mean look as we took the guy to the men's jail.

Our tour was finally over. The night shift officers were standing around waiting to be relieved. Word spread about Frank and me taking the guy to the women's jail and giving the matrons a stimulant. They gave us a good razzing. I didn't say anything but did a slow burn as I walked away from them.

98 · ROBERT J. MORRISSEY

I got about five hours sleep, grabbed something to eat and drove to the bus that was taking the Toledo Tornadoes football team to Jackson Penitentiary to play the prisoners. Naturally the prison team always played at home. I walked up to the coach who was standing by the door to the bus. "Coach, I want to play defense along with my quarterback position today."

"What's the matter with you? Are you a glutton for pain? Did you forget we're playing the prisoners?"

"No, I know who we're playing." I explained what had happened about the guy we took to the women's jail. "I just want to hit someone hard, to release some tension."

He laughed. "Okay."

The bus stopped in front of the prison. A large sign met us. "Jackson Penitentiary, The Largest Walled Prison In The World." It looked like a huge castle made out of old dirty gray bricks. The walls that connected to the building were high and extended as far as I could see. Guards with rifles walked on top. We entered through a large metal door. As soon as the whole team got inside, the door was slammed and locked. We were escorted down a long hall by a guard to a room where we were X-rayed to see if we had any weapons. After we were checked, we went through numerous other doors that were locked behind us. We finally made it to the locker room and we dressed for the game.

Two smiling inmates were in the room. They told us they were there to assist us.

They assisted us all right, but I think their primary purpose was to psychologically prepare us for the game. They kept repeating how their team was undefeated and how other teams were scared to come in here to play. One said, "You don't have anything to worry about, if you get busted up here. We have our own hospital right inside these walls. The doctors are experienced treating guys for broken noses, arms, and legs." I thought, boy, you're an encouraging son of a gun.

Our team got dressed and congregated by the door. The two inmates opened it and shouted, "Follow us." We ran out and there in front of us was a football field complete with stands. We started to run for the field but stopped when we heard a loud roar erupt all around us. Doors banged open and hundreds of prisoners ran out and engulfed us. They, like their buddies, who were with us shouted nice things like how mean their team was and how much business the hospital got from these games. We made it onto the field and had a short warm up and stood on the sideline. Jackson Penitentiary's team rushed out onto the field. I had never seen so many players on one team. There must have been more than a hundred men. There was a complete team in green uniforms. Another team wore blue uniforms. A white team and a blue and gold team. We learned later that Michigan State and the University of Michigan gave their old football uniforms to the prison.

I wasn't impressed by how many players they had on their team. They could only play eleven at a time. I looked behind and noticed a prisoner in the stands staring at me. I didn't pay him any attention. I just wanted to get this game going so I could bang someone and release some tension.

Music sounded and the prison band, dressed in white shirts and denim pants, marched to the middle of the field. The prisoners in the stands booed. The band members in unison, turned and raised their middle fingers back at them. The announcer on the P.A system shouted, "All you damn losers stand up for the National Anthem." The band was halfway through the National Anthem and they stopped. They started playing again only it was another song, *If I had the wings of an angel, over these prison walls I would fly.* The bandleader was mad. He started cussing and punched band members. The prisoners in the stands seeing this, cheered. Guards rushed on the field and broke up the ruckus.

The referee blew his whistle for the game to start. We won the coin toss and elected to receive. A halfback and I lined up deep to return the kickoff. The prison kicker put the ball on the tee and waited for the signal to start the game. It was quiet. All at once someone from the stands shouted. "Get number fifty. He's a cop." Everyone in the stadium stared at me. I was the most popular guy in the place. I could not explain the feeling I was experiencing, but I can tell you now why that guy in the stands had been staring at me.

The halfback who was waiting deep with me was laughing. "Hey, Bob, you got a fan." I looked at him and shook my head. I thought, after this game I'll have enough therapy to last a lifetime.

The ball was kicked high in the air and it slowly tumbled down in front of me. I caught it and ran about twenty-five yards before I was brought down by a big prison player. His face was covered by a large tattoo of a dragon. I expected him to slam a forearm into my face. Instead he picked me up and patted me on the back. "How do you like this beat?" I nodded. "Not bad. I guess I'm playing on your field."

He smiled, "In more ways than one."

The game progressed. Both teams settled down to playing a hard game. The score was a deadlock zero to zero late in the fourth quarter. Our coach sent instructions to pass and go for the score. I dropped back in the pocket to throw. I looked down-field and all our receivers were covered. Out of the side of my eye I saw an opening. I decided to run. I was in the open-field. Two prisoners closed in on me. A Toledo Tornado dove and threw a block and chopped both of them down like a sickle cutting grass. I felt a rush of energy as the goal got closer. I made up my mind. I would not be brought down no matter what. I scored and to my surprise the prisoners in the stands cheered and yelled. "Atta boy, cop." I couldn't believe prisoners cheering a policeman in a penitentiary.

We won the game seven to nothing. Everyone of the prison players walked up to our team and shook hands. I learned that day, a good athlete and a sportsman can be found anywhere. Semi-Professional football is said to be one of the roughest games. This prison team was one of the roughest, but also was one of the best and cleanest team I ever played against.

CHAPTER 28
ONE MORE TIME

I t was time... Face it, Bob, the game is over. Those moments of high adrenalin, running into a brightly lit stadium and the cheers of thousands of spectators ringing in your ears, all that was a memory now.

Football was always my passion. I played football since I was seven or eight years old. When I entered high school, my dream was to become a professional; a quarterback like Bobby Layne of the Detroit Lions. My football idol and the ideal quarterback, I watched and studied every move he made on the field. When I heard that he chewed tobacco when he played, I tried it too. I swallowed the wad when I was tackled, and never tried it again.

The dream, hard practice and dogged determination earned me the honor of making the All City Team. Scholarships followed and I chose to stay in my home town and selected the University of Toledo.

Upon graduation, I waited for the professional teams to contact me. None did. My disappointment was staggering. I was overwhelmed by the depressing realization that my dream of playing pro had come to nothing; my days scrambling on the gridiron were finished.

I sent letters to every professional team asking for a try-out. None replied. Discouraged and bitter, I was about to give up when I received a phone call from the coach of the Toledo Tornadoes football team. Coach, Harold Rader, was a great guy. "Bob, we need a quarterback and we'd sure like you to join the Tornadoes. We pay only seventy dollars a game and we travel on an old bus, but you's get lots of exposure and maybe a pro scout will pick you up.

"When's practice?"

"Tomorrow. We'll have you ready to play at Detroit by the end of the week."

It was different playing semi-pro. The guys were older and knew every trick of the game. Some liked to fortify themselves with booze before a game.

We played the prisoners at Jackson Penitentiary in Michigan. It was the largest walled prison in the world. Naturally, we were obliged to play on their field. Hey, that was a hairy adventure, a story in itself.

Our bus was an old Greyhound. Exhaust fumes seeped through the worn floor boards and we reeked of diesel fuel by the time we finally got to the field. I look back now and wonder why we weren't overcome by the fumes.

Years passed and every game was an adventure of some sort, both humorous and exciting, playing for the Toledo Tornadoes. Pro offers never came. Facing thirty, married with two small children, and an officer on the Toledo Police Department, I was reluctant to give up hope. But, I had to face the facts, be realistic. Football was over for me. The dream of playing pro would never happen now.

It was a sad day when I turned in my football equipment to Marve, the manager. He pushed it back to me. "Hey, Bob, keep it. Think it over, make sure you wanna' hang it up. You love the game too much. We need you. What will you do without the excitement?"

I shook my head and he took the equipment reluctantly. "Well, Bob, it was great knowing you. Give me a break when you catch me speeding."

I went out to the practice field and said so long to the coach and to the guys. They tried to talk me into one more game, but my mind was made up. I walked off the field with my heart and my mind spilling over with memories; that game, this game, and always looking forward to the next one; the competition, the crowds, the noise, the butterflies before the kickoff - and the camaraderie of team buddies. I fought with myself not to look back. Sure, my job as a police officer was filled with challenge and excitement, but there was a void; the yearning for the game was always there. I missed the good old days!

One day, my life suddenly changed. My partner and I had to serve a robbery warrant on a felon. We climbed a high, steep flight of steps to a second-floor apartment directly facing the stairway. We knocked on the door and it exploded open. The guy grabbed me by the throat and pushed me backwards. Reflexively I grabbed him around the neck and we both fell onto the stairs. He was on top of me as we started to tumble down. Every time my back made contact with the steps it felt like someone was hitting it with a baseball bat. I managed to twist his body around so that he took the remainder of the pounding, as I rode him like a sled, thumping our way down.

Neither he nor I could move. The ambulance took both of us to the hospital. After three days of therapy, I managed to walk out.

The Department made an appointment for me to see a surgeon. With no patients visible in the plush waiting room, the surgeon quickly escorted me into his office and pulled up my shirt.

Immediately he shouted to his receptionist, "Set up an appointment at St. Vincent's Hospital for Tuesday. We're going to operate on Officer Morrissey."

I looked around the expensively equipped examining room. Without even a proper diagnosis, I was suspicious that he might use my back to pay for his medical expenses. I made as fast an exit as I could under the circumstances.

In a predicament, I had to talk to somebody about my back, someone I trusted. I went to the University of Toledo and sought out my old football trainer, Vic Brenaman. After he examined my back he asked if I could swim.

"Swim? Well, sure, enough to save my life, I guess."

"Then start swimming."

I took Vic's advice and swam every day. I could feel the

pain and stiffness easing. It was working. My back was healing. I became a fanatic about swimming. Whenever I had some spare time - and even if I didn't - I rushed to the pool and swam laps. I liked it. I wanted to just keep on swimming. It became an obsession.

Of course, I wanted to learn more about swimming. I read books, watched videos and talked with swimming coaches always attempting to improve my swimming style.

Two years went by and my back fully recuperated, my love for swimming, continued. Then one day I saw a large sign on the bulletin board at the police station. *Police Olympics - open to any Officer.* Sure, it wasn't football, but now that didn't matter. There was swimming. I signed up to compete. I felt encouraged by the thought I could look forward to a competitive event.

I went to Columbus, Ohio for my first swimming competition. Wearing loose boxer swimming trunks, I walked out onto the pool deck. All the other swimmers were wearing tight-fitting racing trunks. There were a few strange looks and smiles, but I didn't care.

Heck, I came here to swim, not to parade in a fashion show.

I got up onto the starting block and the race was on. I hit the water and my arms and legs were thrashing. I went full speed, baggy trunks and all.

They draped a gold medal around my neck. The following day my picture was in the paper - and I immediately went out and bought a streamlined racing suit.

Winning a gold medal entitled me to compete in the National Police Olympics in Las Vegas. The winners were culled from among the best police officers in the United States. That winner would be eligible to compete in the International Police Olympics in Australia. Hard work paid off. Wearing my racing brief, I got the win.

I didn't celebrate my success. I practiced harder. The University of Toledo invited me to workout with their swim team. I paid attention to every hint the coach and the college swimmers told me that might help me move faster through the water. I pushed myself to the max.

Australia is known for spectacular scenery, but I had little time for sightseeing. Instead, I swam. I practiced constantly. Sometimes I thought I was sprouting web feet and fins...

With fifty-six men competing in my age group, the final event would bring the best eight men together. These men were tough, strong swimmers, all winners in their countries. I remembered the pep talk my high-school coach gave before a game. "Boys, as you play this game today, remember: You'll be making either a happy memory or one that will haunt you the rest of your life. Do your best and be a winner. Many years in life, you'll look back and smile."

After watching the younger men race, the announcer called on the p.a. system for my group. One of the eight finalists, I was poised on Lane Four. Listening as the various names and countries were called out, I felt an awesome reverence when I heard my name:

"Bob Morrissey representing the United States."

My determination mounted, I vowed I'd dive so far that I'd hit the other end of the pool. I was ready. That old feeling before a football game came back, no one was going to snatch my win from me. My heart was pumping. *One more time, like in the good old days.*

The starting gun sounded and I went off the block like a bullet. I was swimming so fast, the water didn't feel like liquid; it felt like I was flying through air. I didn't look up until I punched the timing pad at the end of the pool. A quick glance, I noticed the other swimmers, like me, were hanging on to the pool ledge, breathing hard. No one knew who won. Then the announcement: "Lane Four the United States. First Place."

I stood on the highest platform with a gold medal around my neck as the band played. *The Star Spangled Banner.* It was the high point of my life.

There's always something more out there if you keep trying, and striving to achieve One more time.

CHAPTER 29
FORTY-FIVE-DOLLAR CANNON BALL

Hazel and Molly shared a room at an expensive motel where their union held a convention. Molly was a big woman who worked on the shipping dock at the factory. She didn't have any trouble lifting heavy cargo. As she entered the room she yelled out to Hazel. "Wait till the men see me this year." She pointed to her head. "This hairdo cost me forty-five-dollars. I'll dazzle them fools. What do you think?"

Hazel clapped her hands. "You'll drive them crazy, Molly. I saw a few check in and there's some pretty good-looking ones. We'll have a chance to meet them later. There's going to be a short meeting and a dance afterwards."

Molly smiled. "I'm ready, this is going to be the night. I can't miss with this forty-five-dollar hairdo. Those dudes will be standing in line to dance with me. Molly became serious. "Hey, why you got your bathing suit on?"

"I'm going down to the pool and relax for awhile; after all the money I paid to stay here, I might as well get some use out of the facilities. I saw a huge whirlpool and I'm going to sit in it and take it easy until the meeting."

"That sounds like a great idea. Wait a minute, I'll put my suit on and we'll go together."

The women entered the large room. They tossed their towels on the deck chairs. Hazel pointed to the huge whirlpool built into the floor. Molly let Hazel lead the way. "You go in first Hazel, and get situated then I'll come in, that way you won't get water on my forty-five-dollar hairdo."

Hazel walked down the steps into the swirling warm water. With ooh's and ah's, she sat in the comforting water. Molly watched and when she was sure there wouldn't be any chance she'd be splashed, she cautiously walked down the steps on her tip toes. Her hands were out to her sides to make sure she had her balance so not to slip and wreck her expensive hairdo. When her foot reached the bottom, she walked to the far end, away from the steps for fear someone entering or leaving might accidentally kick up some water.

The soothing water relaxed the women as they sat back and enjoyed. The only movement from either of them was when Molly saw someone enter or leave the whirlpool. She defensively put her head back and held her hands over her hair, umbrella fashion.

Hazel nudged Molly in the ribs with her elbow. "Look, coming this way; those are the guys I saw check in this morning."

"Yeah, I saw 'em too. I hope they're single." The men entered the whirlpool, sat down and smiled at the women. They were ready to say something when a loud bang sounded. Everyone looked at the direction it came from. The door of the steam room had exploded open and a heavyset bearded guy with a beer belly ran out with a cloud of steam following him. One of the guys in the whirlpool laughed. "Hey, that's Crazy Charlie."

The other guy stood, cupped his hands around his mouth and shouted. "Hellooo, Crazy Charlie."

The big guy's head turned toward the whirlpool. He took a big swig from the can of beer he was holding, let out a loud belch and shouted, "Here comes, Charlie." He put his head down and ran for the whirlpool like a charging bull. His feet made loud slapping sounds as they struck the tile floor.

Molly saw him coming. "Aw, shit." She quickly turned and tried to climb out. The wall was too high and she slipped back into the water. She turned and saw the big guy in the air holding his knees together and his body was folded up like a huge cannon ball. She screamed, "Get away from me, you son-of-a-bitch."

Too late, the water engulfed him and the concussion of his large body exploded water in every direction.

Molly saw the wave coming. She tried to find a place to hide. There was none. Her hands immediately went to protect her forty-five-dollar hairdo but to no avail. The wall of water struck her in the face and chest. It knocked her backwards and underwater. She immediately jumped up cussing and pushing the limp hair out of her face. "Where's he at? I'll kill you, you drunken bastard."

Crazy Charlie surfaced right in front of her. He yelled, "Yeaah, all rightee." He lifted the beer can to his mouth. Molly's fist hit him in the right ear. The beer can flew six feet in the air and Crazy Charlie was knocked underwater. He sprang up coughing, cussing and thrashing the water. "Who's the sneaky jerk who sucker-punched me? I'll break his damn neck." It didn't take him long to find out. A big woman was standing over him in a prize fighter's stance. She swung again and it glanced off his forehead.

"What goes with you big broad? Are you nuts?"

Molly swung again. "I'm going to bust your hollow head, you drunken fool." They both lunged at each other and the war was on.

The two men jumped up and tried to intervene, only to be struck by misguided punches from Crazy Charlie and Molly.

Hazel was concerned for her friend and she leaped on Crazy Charlie's back. The cursing, yelling and the sounds of punches hitting heads and bodies echoed throughout the large room. The fight was at its peak.

A man watched in disbelief then ran to the front desk screaming, "You better call the cops, you got a riot going on in your whirlpool." The manager grabbed the phone and dialed the police.

The dispatcher shouted. "Units 18 and 19. Peaceful Motel, large fight. Take it lights and siren. Step it up. Sounds like a bad one."

CHAPTER 30
THE EPIDEMIC

Captain Elliot came out of his office and threw an assignment paper on my desk. "Bob, hurry, get over to Elm School, they have some type of epidemic going on."

I squinted at him. "An epidemic, what kind of epidemic?"

"It seems the whole school has diarrhea and it's sounds pretty bad."

"Captain, is that a problem for the police, people with diarrhea? I think that's a matter for a doctor, or the health department. I don't know what I can do for someone with the runs. The only thing I know about that subject is when I was in the army they called it the G.I.'s.

"Bob, just get over there now and see if you can assist them."

I smiled. "Captain tell me how to assist someone with diarrhea?"

He got serious. "Get the hell over there, now. I want to know what's going on." I was going to answer with a smart remark till I saw the frown on his face.

The parking spots in front of the school was filled with cars of parents picking up their children. I double parked and ran into the school. Children were lined up in front of the rest rooms. They were fidgeting, squirming and yelling, "Hurry up." The principal was trying to keep order. I walked up to him and showed my badge.

"Officer, I'm glad to see you. We have a real problem here. I don't understand what's going on. Around nine-thirty this morning the children started running to the restrooms. I don't know what caused it." He wanted to continue talking but he started wiggling and ran into the restroom. In a short time he returned. "I'm sorry officer, it's got me too." He shouted to a teacher and told her to take his place directing traffic to the restrooms. "Come on officer, let's go to my office.

I sat down and Principal Hays excused himself again and went into his private restroom. When he came out, he stood next to the restroom door. "I'll just stand here." He continued telling what was going on. "I have the health department, the gas company, and the clean air organization here. Can you think of anyone else I should call?"

"No, Sir, not that I'm aware of. This is my first experience with a call like this. Do you have any idea what might have caused this?"

"No, it started around nine-thirty this morning. I just finished talking with a second grader about a disturbance he caused in class when this mess started."

"What did the boy do?"

"He cussed Santa Claus out in a loud voice in front of the class. He used foul four letter words and the teacher sent him to me. I talked with him and took him back to class. That's when this erupted.

"Principal Hays, this is something I've never dealt with. I don't know where to start. Maybe if I talk with the young boy."

"Okay, officer, I'll get him."

In a short time he returned with a thin, short, red headed boy with freckles all over his face. His clothes were faded and frayed. Principal Hays pointed to a chair in front of me and the young boy sat down with his head bowed. He looked at me through his eyebrows. Principal Hays patted him on the shoulder. "Officer, this is Patrick Morgan." I extended my hand and Patrick slowly extended his and we shook.

"Patrick, I'm Detective Morrissey, I'm glad to meet you." He didn't say anything and I could sense he was scared.

Principal Hays broke the silence. "Officer, I have to check

to see how things are going. If you need me, I'll be in the halls."

Patrick continued to be silent. I took out my badge and put it in his hand. "Did you ever see a detective's badge, Patrick? I'm a policeman but I don't wear a uniform." Patrick kept studying the badge and rubbing it. I kept talking to him and in a short time he spoke and even smiled.

I asked him about the problem he had in class earlier. He shouted. "I went to see Santa Claus before Christmas. I was cold and all I asked him for was a coat and a pair of shoes." He raised his legs so I could see the bottom of his shoes. The soles had large holes worn through them. He took them off and pulled out pieces of cardboard from the insides. He held up a piece of cardboard. "My mother puts this inside so it will help keep me warm. All I wanted was a pair of shoes without holes and a coat. The no good bastard lied to me. He didn't give me nothing. My teacher got mad when I told her this and she sent me to Mr. Hays."

I stared at the worn out tennis shoes with the large holes in the soles. A lump formed in my throat. I was lost for words. I tapped him on the knee. "Don't worry Patrick, I'll see to it that you get a new coat and shoes."

A big smile came across his face. He pushed a large brown paper bag he was holding in front of me. "Here, have some."

"No thank you Patrick, I'm not hungry. You keep your lunch and eat it later."

He shook his head. "This ain't my lunch. It's gum. Take all you want."

I took the bag and looked inside. There was hundreds of small white squares. I looked at Patrick. "What are these?"

"It's gum, Chicklets. After Christmas I went back to the store to tell Santa Claus he was a lying son-of-a-bitch but he was gone. When I left the store there was a big box by the door. I took it and when I got home I opened it and there were a lot of small boxes with gum in it. I emptied the boxes and put the gum in my bag. "

"Patrick did you give any of this gum away?"

"Yeah, everybody who wanted some. I let them take handfuls for their friends."

"Did you give Principal Hays some?"

"Yeah, I gave him some this morning."

I reached down into the bag and swirled my hand around. I pulled out a small empty package. My eyes widen. It didn't say Chicklets. It said Feenamint laxative gum.

CHAPTER 31
SAVE A MARRIAGE

Helen heard the door slam. She rolled over and looked at the clock next to the bed. *Eleven o'clock, it gets later every night.* When she first married Bill he came home right after work. Now he stops every night at the bars and drinks until he can't hold anymore. She knows if she goes downstairs and asks where he was, there will be a big argument. She waited fifteen minutes then decided to go down. She was afraid he fell asleep and had been smoking. She slowly descended the steps and peeked into the front room. Bill was sound asleep snoring in his overstuffed chair. His head was cocked to one side. His metal construction helmet still on his head. His arms were limp and draped over the sides. She noticed his shirt was ripped. She thought, he must have been in another bar room brawl. Slowly she turned feeling depressed, and went back upstairs to bed.

In the morning, Bill raised his large body from the chair. He shook his head a few times, coughed and wobbled into the bathroom. He grabbed a bottle of aspirin and shook it. He cursed when the cotton wouldn't release the pills.

She heard him and thought, when they first were married she would be up to cook his breakfast. Not now, though. He would be mean from the hangover. She waited until she heard the door slam and then went downstairs. All day she pondered what had gone wrong. Was it her fault that Bill was acting this way? She kept thinking for a solution to the problem and went to her best friend's home. She explained to Mary about Bill not coming home from work and going into the bars. Mary listened then smiled.

"Helen, you got to put some zing into your marriage. Buy yourself a sexy dress. Cook a nice dinner. Fill the refrigerator with beer. Go to the video store and get a couple of those double X-rated movies. That ought to turn old Bill on."

Helen was smiling when she left Mary's home. She did everything Mary said except renting the dirty movie. She was nervous about picking out that type of show. She finally built up enough courage and went to the video store. The X- rated movies were in a separate room in the back of the store. She eased her way through the store always looking around to see if she recognized anyone. She was shaking and ran into the room and grabbed two videos without looking at the titles. She walked quickly to another part of the store and picked out another movie. She put this one on top of the X- rated videos and walked to the cashier hoping he wouldn't look at the titles of the dirty ones.

Once at home she called Bill at work and told him to come right home after work because it was very important. He grumbled a little, then said he would.

Helen cooked the meal. She put on her new sexy dress and cooled the beer. Bill came in and shouted. "What the hell is so important?" He looked at his wife and his eyebrows raised. She grabbed his hand and guided him to the table and sat him down. She placed a bottle of expensive beer in front of him. He kept staring with his mouth open. His eyes followed her every move. She put a plate of his favorite food in front of him. She felt a warm feeling come over her when he smiled. She lit the two candles and Bill nodded slightly.

They ate the delicious meal and Helen grabbed Bill's hand and walked him to his recliner. He sat down and she rubbed his shoulders. "I'll be back in a minute." She returned with a can of beer. She grabbed one of the videos and slid it into the VCR. "I'm going to clean up the kitchen. Bill, enjoy yourself. I'm sure you'll love the movie. If you want anything just yell."

Bill nodded and tried to figure out what was going on.

Helen was in the kitchen humming and cleaning up. She thought, Mary, you sure were right. I should have done this a long time ago. Everything was going as planned until Bill's construction helmet flew into the kitchen. He shouted, "You bitch, what you trying to prove? You think I'm funny? I ought to throw this damn television into the street."

Helen ran to the front room. Bill was standing in the middle of it screaming. His finger was shaking and pointing at the TV.

Helen's eyes widened. On the screen were two men without any clothes on. She couldn't believe what they were doing. Bill's face was beet red and his eyes wide open. "You trying to tell me that I'm that way? Is that what this is all about?"

She ran to the TV and ejected the video. She looked at the title. *Secret Love Affair of a Gay Man.*

The neighbor heard the commotion and called the police. "Officer, you better come to 1100 York St. It sounds like the guy next door has gone berserk."

CHAPTER 32
HE MADE IT

I had some wonderful experiences while working as the athletic director of the Toledo Boys Club. One, I will never forget involved a little boy who had the odds against him. His home life was terrible. He wore the same tattered clothes everyday. They was all he had. He was nine years old and could swear like a drunken sailor. The first time I saw Jimmy Bowers he was standing in the shallow end of the swimming pool. His arms resting on the deck. He stayed in that position for hours watching the other boys swim.

I was the swimming instructor that day. When I was in the pool I'd carry a soft volleyball and when a fight erupted, I'd throw the ball and hit the one who started it.

The boys knew if they were hit with the ball, that was their first warning. If they acted up again they were out of the pool for the rest of the day.

I walked around the pool about six times and saw this young boy holding onto the side. I bent down and said, "Hey, kid, why don't you come to swimming lessons? You'll be able to swim like those guys."

He looked up with squinted eyes, blond hair hanging over his face. "Why don't you screw off and mind your own goddamn business."

I was tempted to reach down and grab him by the hair and pull him out of the water and throw him out of the pool. Instead I laughed inside. I liked the kid's spirit. I stared at him. He glared back at me. I bounced the ball off his head and started walking the deck again.

From that day on he was in the pool everyday, always positioning himself in the water with his arms resting on the deck. He stayed in that spot. His face never got wet. I walked the deck and every time I'd pass him, I dropped the ball on his head. One time I ignored him and didn't drop the ball. I passed by, then looked back. He appeared rejected. I quickly turned and popped him in the head with the ball. I shouted, "Gotcha" His face lit up with laughter. I continued to walk the deck. The young boy's eyes followed me the rest of the period.

The next day at swimming lessons, I looked into the crowd of boys in the water and I saw the little guy. He tried to hide in the group. I didn't pay any attention to him. I got in the water and explained that the first thing we had to learn was to put our heads underwater and hold our breath. I ducked under and came up. I pointed at the boys. "Now, you guys drop your heads under like I did." Everyone in the class put his head under except Jimmy. He puckered up his face and closed his eyes. He bent forward, but his head wouldn't go under. He tried again, but couldn't get his head under.

I made my way through the water to him. He saw me coming and he raised his arms. "I don't need your bullshit. I can do it myself."

Hands on my hips I said, "Okay, big shot, you swear pretty good, but you're scared to stick your head underwater. You're chicken."

A mean look came over his face. His head quivered, and he immediately forced his head under. I tapped him on the head, "Now, that's better." He smiled and he went under again. He kept ducking. I shouted, "That's great son, but we've got to get on to the next steps."

He smiled and looked determined. "I can do this shit. Tell me what to do and I'll do it."

Days passed and Jimmy never missed a swimming lesson. He learned every step. I noticed this kid was different from the others. He learned fast and was a natural swimmer.

When his arms entered the water on the crawl stroke they

went in like knife blades with no splash. His flutter kick looked like an outboard motor. His streamlined body glided through the water with hardly any resistance. The boy was a diamond in the rough.

One day I asked Jimmy, "Would you help me teach swimming lessons? You're a great swimmer, and I think you could help the other boys. You get in the water and I'll stand on the deck. I'll explain to the boys what I want them to do. You will show them what I mean. Will you do it?"

"You're shitting me, Bob. You really mean it?"

"Yes, I mean it. Will you do it?"

His expression was full of excitement. "Sure, I'll do it. What else do you want me to do?"

"Well, if you're going to be an instructor, you've got to quit swearing. Can you stop swearing?"

"Hell yes, I can quit. I promise, I won't swear anymore."

Jimmy never missed a swimming class. The boys got into the water and leaned against the side of the pool. I would explain how to glide, kick and pull their arms, and Jimmy would demonstrate. The boys stared with amazement while the young boy swam. They praised him and asked questions. One day a group asked him, "When are we going to get as good as you?"

He said, "Keep your goddamn mouths shut and listen to what Bob says and you'll be good." He looked up at me. He knew he said something wrong. He put up his hands. "I won't do it again."

The Junior Olympics games were coming up in a month. The youngest age group was for twelve-year-olds. Jimmy watched the swim team practice every day. He studied everything they did. When it was open swim he imitated their form. I made a phone call to a friend who worked for the City Recreation Department. I explained to him about my nine-year-old swimmer. I asked if I could enter him in the twelve-year-old group. He gave me the okay, but warned the young boy would get his ears pinned back. I told him I understood, but I thought it would be a good learning experience for the young swimmer.

Jimmy practiced with the swimming team. He worked hard and had the desire to be a winner. I explained to him he would be competing against older boys. He shrugged his shoulders, "It don't matter, Bob."

The day of the swimming meet, I took the old bus and drove my team to the city pool. When we got off the bus, I noticed parents were bringing their children to the pool with them and taking seats in the stands. None of my boys' parents were there.. Gathering them in a group, we locked hands. I said, "We're in this together. This is our team, and we're going to pull for each other."

A familiar voice from the group, "We're going to kick their asses." I didn't say anything to Jimmy; I felt it was a nervous reaction.

The swimming meet started. Jimmy sat as close to the pool as he could. He studied the swimmers. His group was called to the starting blocks. I tapped him on the head. "Jimmy, remember everything we practiced. Relax, and do your best." He turned to me and squeezed my hand.

I watched him climb onto the starting block. He was so much smaller than the other boys. I wondered if I had made a mistake entering him in the older group. Jimmy showed no sign of being nervous. He threw his small chest out and rotated his arms like propellers. I was uneasy and nervous. I watched the swimmers dive off the blocks. Jimmy hit the water perfectly and was out in front. I thought the bigger boys would catch up to him. The little guy didn't slow down. Halfway through he was still ahead. The race looked like a flock of geese flying in their V formation. Jimmy was the leader. He increased his lead and won by a body length. I rushed to him, reached down and pulled him from the water. He looked up at me and was breathing hard, "Did I do all right, Bob? I did what you told me."

"You were perfect. You're my champ. I'm proud of you."

Jimmy swam against the winners of the other heats. This boy was determined. He won first place in the twelve-year-old division and was awarded a gold trophy. He held that trophy all the way back to the club. When someone asked if they could see it, he'd say, "Just look; don't touch it." Jimmy didn't run home like the other boys who won trophies to show their parents their prizes. He hung around the club until it closed. I didn't question why he didn't go home. I could tell something was bothering him.

A few days later a lady came to the Boys Club. She asked if she could talk with me. She then told this story. "Jimmy is a student of mine. The boy has been constant trouble. He doesn't know who his father is. His mother is selling her body and is a drug, and alcohol abuser. Any good the school system does for the boy is destroyed when he gets home. He has a foul mouth and is constantly disrupting the class. Everyday he gets into fights."

I looked at her and shook my head. "I understand, but how does that affect me?"

"Well, a couple days ago Jimmy came to school and would not take off his coat. I went to his desk and ordered him to remove it. I was ready to send him to the principal because I felt he was going to start cussing. Slowly, he removed it. He had a beautiful swimming trophy hidden under his coat. I nearly made the most terrible mistake of my life. I almost asked, 'Where did you steal this?' I caught myself.

Jimmy pointed at the trophy and showed where his name was engraved on it. This was the first time I ever saw the child smile. He was so proud. I asked him about it, and he told me the whole story. I placed his trophy on my desk so the whole class could see it. Since this happened, the boy has changed. He asked if he could leave the trophy on my desk. I told him as long as he wanted there, it would stay. I just wanted to tell you thanks for taking the time with him."

I was puzzled. "Thanks? That little guy made me a happy man."

****

Later I was appointed to the police department. Between raising a family and the job, I lost track of Jimmy. Twenty-five years later I was working as a detective. The desk sergeant called me over the intercom. "Bob, there's people here to see you." I walked to the front desk and there stood a neatly dressed couple with a small child. The man smiled and held out his hand. Right away I recognized Jimmy. He still had that cocky, determined expression. He shook my hand and then looked to his wife.

"Mary, this is the man I told you so much about. Bob, this is my wife, Mary, and my little girl, Sandra. After you left the Boys Club, I kept on swimming. I got a scholarship for swimming and went to college. I earned a degree in engineering and have a good job." He then showed me pictures of his home. He looked back at his wife. "I'll never forget Bob."

A warm feeling came over me. It was hard to talk. I tapped him on the head and said, "You made me a happy man, Jimmy. I wondered about you a lot. I'll never forget how you took on those older swimmers and won." We talked for a while. When he was leaving, I asked, "How's the language? Have you learned any new words?" He shook his head, smiled and waved goodbye..

CHAPTER 33
FISHING

"Unit 20 is back in service." Officer McNae put the mike back in the cradle. He looked at his partner who was driving. "Mike, do you realize that was the eighth disturbance call we went on in the last two hours? It must be a full moon tonight."

"It don't have to be a full moon. Today is payday and it's Friday night. They get liquored up and think they're having a good time kicking the hell out of each other."

"Well I don't care about their good times. Those calls worked up an appetite. Let's go to some quiet restaurant and get something to eat."

"At this hour, there's no quiet restaurant. Every place will be loaded with drunks. You won't be able to enjoy your meal. Let's go to the back of Johnny's place. I'll talk to the cook in the kitchen and he'll fix us something to go. We'll park down by the river and eat in the car."

"Great idea. Most of the drunks are in the restaurants. We won't have to deal with them by the water."

Mike parked the car by the noisy exhaust fan behind the restaurant. McNae went inside and in a short time came out with two bags. Mike leaned over and opened the door for him. McNae handed the bags to his partner. "Let's get out of here before we get a call."

Mike laughed. "You know this job is like delivering milk. We know on Friday nights we're going to be sent to the same homes. They never seem to learn."

"Well, look at it this way. If it wasn't for those idiots, we wouldn't have a job."

"Yeah, I guess you're right."

The car bounced a little when it went off the paved road. Mike parked the car next to the river. "Now isn't this nice and quiet. This is the way to eat. It seems like every time I go in a restaurant with this uniform on someone comes up and starts a conversation. One time some mother dragged her son to me. She pointed at me and said. 'You see this policeman. If you don't eat your food he'll arrest you and put you in jail.' The kid's eyes got real big and I think he crapped his pants."

"Yeah, I had that happen to me too. No wonder kids are afraid of us."

Both men were eating their meal. All at once a fisherman lit a lantern. "Hey Mike, now we can enjoy our food and watch that guy pull in a big fish."

Mike watched the silhouette of the fisherman next to the light. He got quiet and McNae asked. "Hey, Mike, what's the matter?"

"You ain't going to believe this. That guy fishing. He's not throwing his line in the water."

"Where the hell is he throwing it?"

"He's throwing it in the bushes."

McNae leaned over and looked. "He probably made a bad cast."

"No, this is the fourth time he did it. I'm going over there and see what he's up too."

"Hey, wait a minute. Let's finish our meal. That wacko will probably turn on and we'll have to do battle. I just want to finish eating."

In a short time McNae squeezed the paper that had been wrapped around his sandwich. He threw it into the empty bag then took a last drink from his coffee. "We'll get out of the car with no noise and come up behind him. Make sure he doesn't go for his tackle box. He's probably got a big knife inside."

It was an eerie sight seeing the guy in the bright flickering light casting his line into the bushes. The officers stopped about five feet from him. Mike coughed. "Sir."

The man's head swung around. "Hush, I've got a bite."

The officers looked at each other and shrugged their shoulders. Mike was about to talk again when he was interrupted by a loud screech. A large rat exploded out of the bushes with a hook in his mouth and was headed right for the officers. They jumped and the rat ran under them. McNae shouted. "Holy cow, the damn fool's got a rat hooked. Don't get bit by that thing, they're full of disease."

The rod was bent and the guy kept reeling the rat in. When it got close to him, he dispatched it with a baseball bat. The officers slowly walked back to the man and stared at him. McNae squinted "You do this very ofter?"

"Oh, about twice a week."

"How many times you been bit?"

"Never, when they get close, I give them a good lick with this bat."

"Why don't you just fish for fish like normal people do? You won't have to worry about getting bit."

"Well, I'll tell you officers, rats fight a lot harder than fish. I have no competition, no one else fishes for rats and there is a good supply of them."

The officers walked away shaking their heads. McNae said, "Mike, would you call that guy a ratterman?"

Mike raised his eyebrows. "Lets get back to normal patrol."

CHAPTER 34
SUCKER PUNCHED

The painters were bent over stirring paint with wooden paddles. Curtis squinted through his blood shot eyes, hurting from the bright morning sunlight and a hangover. Leon, the other man looked at him. "Man, you better shut them eyes or you'll bleed to death. Why don't you go home at night and sleep instead of drinking?"

Curtis stood up and pointed his paddle at him. "You listen, fool, you can tell me what to do on this job but when I get off, I'll do what I want to do. Understand?"

Leon gave him a stern look but didn't say anything. He knew he had a full days work ahead of him and didn't want any trouble. He began to stir the paint again. Curtis continued to glare at Leon. Slowly, he put his paddle back in the bucket and stirred. Leon went to the truck and got a large drop cloth and when he returned he saw the familiar looking bottle come out of Curtis's pocket. Curtis raised the bottle to his mouth.

"Hey, man, you ain't drinking that stuff when you're working for me. I want the paint to go on the building right." He grabbed the bottle and the neck raked across Curtis's teeth. Curtis's hand felt his mouth to check if his teeth were still there. His other hand clenched into a fist and he lunged at Leon. Leon raised the wine bottle over his head. "You come one step closer and I'll break it over your skull."

Curtis stopped dead in his tracks. "Man, wait, don't break that bottle, it's all I got and I don't have money to buy another."

"Just back off and nothing will happen to the bottle. You

can have it back after we're done. Do you understand?" Curtis mumbled a few choice words, picked up his paint can and brush and walked toward the building. He stopped and looked back.

"Listen, you rotten low life. I'm going to start at the far end of this building and you go to the other end. I don't want you near me. If you come closer, I'll break your damn head. Do you hear?"

"You better believe I hear. There's no way I want to work next to a winehead."

"Who you calling a winehead, fool? He threw his brush down and rushed to where Leon was standing and pointed his finger at him. "What did you call me?"

"You're a drunk aren't you?"

I may be a drunk but I'm not a winehead."

Leon squinted and shook his head, "What's the difference a drunk or a winehead?"

Curtis shouted, "A drunk has class and a winehead doesn't. Understand? You ever call me a winehead again we're going to get down and find out who the best man is. I'm warning you, Leon, you keep that smart talk to yourself."

Leon kept telling himself to keep cool and hoped they could get the job done without a fight. "Okay, Curtis, I won't call you a winehead again. Let's get this work done." Curtis went back to the far end of the building, mumbling and cussing.

The day passed and they progressively got closer to one another. Nasty things were mumbled about each other while they painted. When they heard these remarks they gave each other threatening looks. Leon put his brush down. "I think we better paint that big overhead door now. Tell the guy inside to open it."

Curtis glared at him, then walked to a small door and knocked. No response from inside. He drew back his leg and kicked. He continued to kick and yell. Finally a voice inside shouted. "What the hell's the matter with you? What do you want?"

"Open the garage door, fool." Curtis glanced at Leon who was shaking his head and looking disgusted. Curtis shouted, "Man, now what the hell's the matter with you?"

"Just a little while ago you were talking about class, now you go and kick that door and call the guy who you never saw a fool. Man, you just don't understand."

"Don't worry how I act or talk, the damn door is going up, ain't it?"

The huge door went up in jerks as the ancient motor strained and squealed trying to pull the big door open. A man inside stood in disbelief looking at the two men arguing when the door went up. Leon saw the man and he stopped. Curtis continued. A large semi truck pulled into the driveway and Curtis's voice was drowned out by it's noisy engine. He shook his head, picked up his brush and went back to painting the door frame.

The truck motor continued to idle and vibrations could be felt on the pavement and the door frame. As fate would have it the large spring holding up the door was loose. The constant trembling from the engine caused it to loosen more. A loud bang, and it let go. The weight from the huge door caused it to drop at a terrific speed. Curtis heard something, turned his head and was struck flush on the chin by the door. The door hit the ground, rebounded and struck Curtis again under his chin. He flew backwards and landed on his back. The paint bucket dropped on his chest spilling paint all over him.

Curtis jumped up and shook like a dog trying to get the paint off. He threw his brush at Leon. "You sucker punched me, you bastard. Now let's see how tough you are." He grabbed Leon by the neck and punched him in the face. "I'll teach you to be sneaky and sucker punch me. I ought to kill you."

Leon didn't know what happened. He did know he had to defend himself. He started punching Curtis in the stomach. He shouted, "I had enough of you. I'll beat you to a pulp." The two men locked into hand to hand combat and were rolling all over the driveway.

132 · ROBERT J. MORRISSEY

"Unit 20, this is the dispatcher. Go to 1210 Monroe street. Two men fighting. Better step it up, sounds like a good one." The scout car turned onto the 1000 block of Monroe street and cars were bumper to bumper. The officers turned on the overhead red lights and siren. Cars squeezed over to open a path so the police car could get through. When the officers got in front of 1210 Monroe, the two combatants were in the middle of the street fist fighting and swearing.

One of the officers pointed at Curtis. "Look at that guy, he's covered with paint." They ran from the scout car and pulled the fighters apart.

One of the officers yelled, "What's going on here? Why are you fighting?"

Curtis hollered, "All day this fool has been hassling me. I stayed clear of the jerk and when he got close, he punched me twice. Man, he sucker punched me. I didn't do anything to him."

The officers looked at Leon. "What's your story?"

"I was painting. I heard him yell and sees he's covered with paint. He throws his brush at me and charges like a wild man, swinging his fists. Officers, I think that wine has shrunk his brain. He's nothing but a crazy winehead."

When Curtis heard this, he broke free from the officer holding him and swung at Leon. "I told you never to call me that." The officers pulled them apart again.

A man shouted from the driveway. "Officers I saw the whole thing. I opened the overhead door. That door hasn't been opened for years. The spring is old and must of broke and the door crashed down." He pointed at Curtis. "It hit him on the chin and then it bounced back up and got him again. I believe he thought the other guy punched him."

The officers walked Curtis and Leon back to the building. They examined the door and saw the large spring hanging down. One of the officers looked at Curtis and Leon. "You guys are lucky that heavy door didn't come down on your heads. It would of squashed you like a grape. Thank the Lord you're alive." Leon and Curtis's eyes opened wide and they nodded at each other.

Leon walked to his jacket and got the bottle of wine he took from Curtis earlier. He looked at the officers. "Is it all right if I give him this? I think he needs it." The officers smiled and nodded.

Curtis unscrewed the cap and then handed the bottle back to Leon. "I think you need a drink, too." Leon grabbed the bottle and took a big swig. They both sat down next to each other with their backs leaning against the building and began to finish off the bottle.

The officers looked at each other and one said, "I don't think we're needed here anymore."

CHAPTER 35
INGENIOUS

I t was my first full week working the new district. We had to hit off at a call box on the street at six thirty in the morning. After working all night your eyes do tricks on you. The call box was located in a neighborhood that consisted of small businesses. I noticed a couple of times while we were waiting, a hand would come up from a window of the basement of a machine shop. It then pushed the grate in the sidewalk up and placed a neatly wrapped box on the sidewalk. The hand would then put the grate back in place.

The package stayed on the sidewalk for a short time then a man walking by looked down at it, turned around to see if anyone was looking, then he quickly bent and grabbed the small package and put it under his coat and went on his way.

The next day the same thing happened, only this time an elderly woman picked it up and quickly walked away. My partner, Ben, asked. "Bob, are you seeing the same thing I am? Every morning that hand comes up from that window and puts a package on the sidewalk. It happens almost at the exact time. I wonder if they're pushing drugs out of that machine shop."

"Yeah, I noticed it too. I've been so tired from running all those calls I didn't want to get something started at hit-off-time. I think we ought to do something about it. What do you say, I get next to that grate tomorrow and when that hand comes up with the package I'll grab it and hold it. You run in the place and see who I got."

"Good idea."

The next morning I eased my back against the front of the building and looked down at the basement window. Sure enough the window came open and the hand pushed the grate up. I grabbed the guy by the wrist. I shouted, "I've got him, Ben. Hurry, get in there and see who it is."

A voice shouted from the window below. "Hey, what the hell you doing? Let my arm go."

Ben yelled, "Bob, turn him loose, I got him."

I quickly ran inside. The guy yelled, " I didn't do anything wrong."

Ben said, "Tell us about it."

He hesitated then said. "Well, every night me and my partner drink a few beers. The boss would raise hell if he found out we were drinking on the job. We don't want him to see the empty cans. We smash them and put them in a box and neatly wrap the box with new brown paper. I put the box on the sidewalk and some would-be thief thinks the box got something valuable inside and they steal it. I'd love to see their faces when they open up the package and see the crushed beer cans."

CHAPTER 36
A LESSON IN HARD KNOCKS

The big day arrived for Jim Murphy and Mike Roe. It was graduation day. The boys were friends for many years. They were noted for their athletic abilities and had played on the same teams since grade school. But next year they'd be separated, they received scholarships to different colleges. They were sitting on Murphy's back porch reminiscing of all the great experiences they had over the years.

Jim looked at his friend. "You know Mike, it's sure going to be strange next year when football season comes around. It will be the first time in many years we aren't on the same team."

"Yeah, I know. It will be strange."

"We should celebrate tonight. After all, it's graduation night and it will probably be the last big thing we do together. We should celebrate like adults."

Mike squinted, "What you talking about?"

"Man, we should get some alcohol for tonight. That's what men do when they celebrate.'

"But I never drank before."

"That's all right, I never did either. I think it's time we do. This is graduation night and that's the right time to start."

Mike agreed and made arrangements to invade his father's whiskey cabinet. When Jim left he looked back and pointed at Mike. "Don't forget to bring - you know what tonight." Mike nodded.

The front of the auditorium was filling up with the

graduating class. They were dressed in black robes and stiff square hats with white tassels hanging over the sides. Everyone was serious and talked in whispers. Jim sat next to Mike. "You didn't forget it, did you Mike?"

"Don't worry I got it stuffed in my belt under this robe."

Everything became quiet. The principal and other teachers took their places on the stage. The first speaker walked to the lectern and looked down at the students. He gave praise to them and kept rambling on. Jim elbowed Mike. "Give me that bottle."

"Are you nuts? You ain't going to start drinking in here."

Jim dropped his hand into Mike's lap and whispered. "Give me the bottle. I can drink the whole thing and it won't affect me."

Mike slowly reached into his robe and placed the bottle in Jim's hand. Jim slid down in his seat, unscrewed the cap and took a big swig of the whiskey. The burning sensation caused him to straighten up and exhale hard. "Whew, that stuff is hot." His breath hit the back of the girl sitting in front of him. She was startled and immediately rubbed the back of her neck and turned around to give him a dirty look. She was shocked when she saw the bottle in Jim's hand. She elbowed the girl sitting next to her and whispered. They both looked at him and he raised the bottle and toasted them.

The boys passed the bottle back and forth until it was empty. When the speeches were done the students were called to the stage to get their diplomas. The whiskey was working on the boys. They tried not to laugh but they couldn't stop. The principal called Jim Murphy's name. "At this time I would like to call Mike Roe to the stage too. These boys made this school proud with their sports skills. They did everything together in sports and I think it's only right if they were called together to receive their diplomas."

People stood and clapped as the two young men made their way to the stage. Jim grabbed Mike's arm. "I"m dizzy what if I fall in that band pit?"

"Don't worry about it. As soon as you get on the stage just

look at the principal and aim for him. Don't take your eyes off him."

The two were now on the stage and the people started clapping again. Mike did a little jig and his hands went over his head like a boxer who had just won the championship. He didn't want to do this but the whiskey was influencing him. Jim seeing Mike do this also raised his arms. The people clapped louder. Mike thought, Man, just let me get off this stage. I have to get control before I do something stupid. They crossed the stage and made it to the principal. The principal again heaped praise on them. Mike took his diploma and tapped the principal on his back. "You ain't seen anything, Pops. Wait till we get in college. We're going to make you real proud."

The principal looked concerned. Mike realized what he had said and he wiped his mouth and quickly walked off the stage and back to his seat.

The ceremony was over and the students gathered in the hall waiting to turn in their caps and robes. A friend of Mike and Jim walked up to them. "Hey, where you guys going now?"

Mike slurred, "We're going to a bar and celebrate. You want to come along?"

"Sure I'd like to. I'll drive. Hey, you guys haven't turned in your stuff."

Mike laughed. "Don't worry about it. We're going to celebrate in our caps and gowns."

They walked out of the school with their graduation clothes on and got in the car. The friend drove to the downtown section of Toledo. Jim pointed to a brightly lit bar. "Hey, there's the place we want to go."

The driver shook his head. "Man, this is skid row. That's the High Way Bar. My dad told me about that place. It's the toughest bar in town. Crazy things happen in there. I'd stay clear of that joint."

Both Mike and Jim insisted that the High Way Bar was where they wanted to go. The three of them walked in. The winos, sailors and iron-workers stared at the caps and gowns the boys were wearing. Mike and Jim ordered whiskey. The other boy didn't want anything. He kept looking around watching the door in case something happened. Mike and Jim got their drinks and they toasted each other. Mike spun around on his bar stool and stared at the people. He meant to whisper, but it came out loud. "You know Jim, I bet we could kick everyones' ass in this dump."

Jim nodded. "I know we could."

The place got quiet and in no time three big men wearing hard hats came up. One of them pointed. "You guys think you're pretty smart all dressed up. You keep talking brave and we'll give you a real lesson. Both Jim and Mike jumped up.

Mike shouted. "We not only talk brave, we are." He took a punch at the biggest one. The guy ducked and than swung back hitting Mike flush on the chin. Mike bounced off the bar and into the guy's arms. The guy grabbed Mike's gown and ripped it down the middle. Mike climbed on top of the bar and dove on the guy. He looked like Batman when the torn gown opened up like a cape. The driver ran out and drove to Jim Murphy's home and told his father. When Mr. Murphy pulled up in front of the bar the police were bringing his son and Mike out. The boys had swollen eyes and bloody noses. Mr. Murphy walked to the police officers. He pointed at his son. "Officers that's my boy. What did he do?"

"He got into a good one and got popped a few times. Him and his friend got their licks in too. We don't know who started it because no one wants to talk about it."

Mr. Murphy shook his head. "Officers, I don't know what made him come to this bar and get involved in this ruckus. These boys have never been in any trouble. They graduated tonight and I can't believe this. That's my wife in the car and she's crying her eyes out. Could we take them home. I'm sure there won't be any more trouble.

The officers nodded and one said, "Okay, but wait here." He went back in the High Way Bar and returned with the two mortar board hats. He put them on the boys heads and opened the back door of Mr. Murphy's car and motioned for the boys to get in. "I hope you guys learned another lesson tonight. From the looks of your father, you're going to get some homework."

Mr. Murphy thanked the officers and assured them there would be homework tonight.

CHAPTER 37
WHAT A DIFF'RENCE A DAY MADE

It's funny how a song can bring back memories from the past. I was listening to my car radio when the song - "What A Diff'rence A Day Made" started playing. Immediately my mind flashed to the past. I was sitting in a neighborhood bar called the Bide Away. A beautiful song, "What A Diff'rence A Day Made" was playing. The words fit my mood that day. The singer Dinah Washington had the perfect voice to sing that song. When the record stopped I got up and walked to the juke box. I reached into my pocket and came out with five quarters. The small sign read five plays for a quarter. I dropped in the five quarters. The juke box acknowledged it got the money by making a clanking sound every time a quarter dropped into the slot. My finger went up and down the glass looking for the song written on the inside. A-4 "What A Diff'rence A Day Made." I pushed the button twenty five times and went back to my stool.

I just stared at my glass and wiped the moisture from the sides of it as that wonderful song played over, and over and over. As the song played on the redundant music caused the guys at the bar to unconsciously move their glasses with the beat of the song. Time went on, and the song continued to play. I was infatuated with it. It had me in a trance. The trance was broken by the loud scraping sound of a stool being pushed away from the bar. I looked in the direction of the noise. A big burly guy about six two was standing up with his hands over his ears. He was screaming. "I can't take that song again." He rushed to where I was sitting and pointed a finger at me. "If you play that song again I'll run your head through that juke box."

I didn't say anything to him but got up and walked to the middle of the bar where the bartender was. I pushed a dollar bill at him. "Give me four quarters." He gave me change and I walked over to the juke box. I dropped the four quarters into the slot and the machine clanked again for me to pick my selections. I started to press A.4 but before I could press it twenty times a loud animal growl came from the direction of the bar. I looked out of the side of my eye and I saw the big guy rushing toward me like a wild bull. I watched him in the reflection of the glass on the juke box. When he got close I jumped to the side. He hit the machine with his big head. The impact caused the arm holding the needle to scrape across the record; With a loud screeching, rasping sound, the juke box went dead.

The big lummox bounced off the juke box and rebounded off the wall. He shook his head and focused. The rush was on again. I waited until he was about three feet away and I planted my feet and threw a punch that hit him flush in the face. The man didn't even blink. He swung a fist the size of a picnic ham and it struck me in the right eye. Fireworks erupted in my head. My body reeled backwards knocking chairs and tables over. I slid under a table. I gained my senses and saw his legs. I quickly crawled out behind him, jumped to my feet and swung a fist to his right ear. This made him groan a little but didn't put him down. I jumped on his back and put one arm in a choke hold around his neck and with my fist I pounded his right ear. He was swinging me like a cape but I managed to hold on and kept punching.

Someone yelled. "The cops are on their way." The big guy ran for the front door. I jumped off his back and ran out the back door like a dog that had been scalded.

I went home and emptied a tray of ice cubes into a towel and put it over my eye. It didn't help much. When I removed it and looked in the mirror my eye was swollen shut. It was black, yellow, and purple.

The next day, before getting on the bus to take our Toledo Tornado football team, to Detroit, I went to the drugstore and bought a pair of dark sun glasses. I picked the ones with the largest lens. I thought the glasses would cover my black eye. They did a pretty good job but the bruise extended down over my cheek bone. The guys saw me coming with the shades on. They started to make wise cracks until they saw the bruise below the glasses. George Wells lifted the glasses. "Wow, who the hell popped you?" He shouted to the other guys. "Hey, look at this shiner." I ignored them and got on the bus without giving any explanation.

On the ride to Detroit the song kept haunting me. We played the preliminary game against the Detroit Rangers. In the main event the Detroit Lions, played the Green Bay Packers. We won our game and a couple of players from the Lions informed us we were invited to a party after their game.

I with the other members of the Toledo Tornadoes, went to the party. It was great being with some of the stars of the National Football League. I was talking to one of these stars, a defensive half back by the name of "Night Train Lane." A lady walked up. I kept staring at her. My intense stare, and the black eye caught her attention. She squinted. "Whew, honey, who did that to your eye?"

I stuttered, and said. "You might of been the cause of it."

"Why me? I've never saw you before."

I told her how much I liked her beautiful song. I explained how I played it so many times it caused a big fight.

She placed both my hands in hers, and stared directly into my eyes. She said. "This is for you." She sang. *What A diff'rence A Day Made.* The large room became quiet. Everyone was staring at us.

She finished the song and I said, "I will never forget this." She smiled, kissed her hand and wiped it on my black eye.

On the ride back to Toledo everyone was asking why Dinah Washington sang that song to me. I told them. "That's our secret."

Monday I went back to the Bide Away. I sat at my usual

stool. I looked down about five seats and saw the big lummox I had the fight with. His left ear was swollen twice the size of normal. Like my eye it was black, blue, purple, and red. He was staring at me in the mirror behind the bar. His fingers were tapping the top of the bar.

My thoughts went back to the beautiful song and how Dinah Washington sang it for me alone. I kept asking myself. Was it a dream? I could still see her as plain as the day she did it.

I remember every expression on her face as the words to that wonderful song came out of her. I jumped up, flagged a dollar bill in my hand and shouted. "Bartender give me four quarters."

* * *

An interesting note to this story. One month later I was appointed to the police department. Needless to say I felt relieved when the interview was over and they didn't ask any questions relating to my black eye and the above story.

CHAPTER 38
WHO WERE THOSE GUYS IN THE MAROON UNIFORMS

I suppose if I weren't a policeman I could tell this story the way I think it really happened, but...I can't bring myself to say that I believe in ghosts. They'd laugh me out of the department. So I'll give you the facts and let you take it from there.

I played football at Woodward High School and for a couple of years under Frosty England at Toledo University and then in service--about seven years in all. Then I found myself out of school and a rookie cop and suddenly faced with the idea that there were no more football games for me to play; I wasn't ready for it. I still needed the challenge, the contact, and the team companionship. Maybe the idea of becoming a spectator hit me as a sign of old age. I didn't like it. I wasn't going to have it.

I soon discovered there were plenty of others like me: Bill Gregus, Lyle Veler, Porter King, Delroy Pryba, Stan Sterger and plenty more. Make a noise like a football and there they were.

That's how the Toledo Tornadoes were born in the1950's. We heard about a semi-pro football league in Michigan and decided to be part of it. Veler and I were selected to contact the league. Two days later we were invited to attend a league meeting in Monroe, Michigan. That's where the trouble started.

They were okay to us ... too good. Next thing you know we had a game booked at Melvindale outside of Detroit and had agreed to post a $500 forfeiture bond against non appearance for a game the following Saturday. We didn't even have a team yet, let alone uniforms, but we had a schedule.

The next day about 30 guys showed up for practice. We had a meeting first and talked about money; the $500 forfeiture bond and $2,000 for uniforms. Suddenly it was the quietest meeting I ever attended. Porter King was doing some figuring and he came up with the idea of everyone chipping in $16.50 to make the bond. It didn't quite work out that way. Some guys had to give more because others could give less, but we finally came up with the money.

We posted the bond in Monroe, but the uniforms turned out to be something else. We tried everything, but we couldn't raise the price of a football or the air to go in it, let alone the price of uniforms. The game was less than six days away and the situation was getting serious, especially with our $500 already posted. That's when this old man came into our lives. Don't ask me from where.

"You boys need uniforms?" He quavered. "I've got a set you can use."

This was crazy. What would an old bird like this be doing with football uniforms?

"I've got them at the house," he went on. "Drive me over there and you can take a look at them."

Well, we had nothing to lose but Lyle's gasoline, so we took him up on his offer.

It was an ordinary house like dozens of others around it. The old man invited us to follow him and slowly he made his way to the second floor and into an attic. There in a neat row were about 25 cardboard boxes. He picked up two of them, wiped away a thin layer of dust, and carried them downstairs. We followed.

He opened a box and held up a deep red jersey with white stripes on each sleeve. It was like something I'd seen in an old Frank Merriwell illustration. There was padding cross-stitched at the shoulders and reinforced leather pads sewed to the elbows. The pants were heavily padded all around and very large and very loose. From a second box he pulled a helmet and unfolded it. This uniform had to be from the 1911 era— early 1911.

I looked at Veler and he looked at me. The old man intercepted the glances and read them better than either of us.

"These uniforms," he quavered, "were worn by the Toledo Maroons and we played the best. We started out just like you, an independent team made up of guys who loved the competition, and played for whatever we could get. It took real men to wear these uniforms."

"Sure, pop, but things have changed. Those uniforms are a little out of style."

"We played in the early pro leagues," he went on. "You know, what is now the National Football League, and we took on the greatest players that schools like Michigan, Ohio State and Notre Dame could produce. And the Carlisle Indians."

I was worried about getting back to practice. The old guy kept rattling off names and teams. Some were familiar. Most were before my time. We backed off and I finally said. "We'll be seeing you, pop. We'll be seeing you."

Lyle and I spent a lot of time in the next days trying to find someone who would equip us; but, man, it just wasn't to be. Time was growing short and we were worried not only about playing football but about losing our $500. Some of that money came from where it never should have been touched, and we just couldn't afford to lose it.

We didn't know what to do. There seemed to be no answer, except every time we looked up, the old guy would be there. Finally we had no choice. We'd wear the antique uniforms.

The old guy watched as we carried them from the attic to the car, box by box. He'd look at the number on the outside of a box and mutter a name–5, Lou Mauder, 13, John Schimmel, 17, Hughie Hackett. We carted the stuff over to the field, the old man with us. It was evident he was going to be wherever his uniforms were.

One look at the gear and immediately all the guys became

stand-up comics. Everybody said he was Jim Thorp or Knute Rockne and made fun of the fact that the pants were so long they could use armholes.

Personally, I was depressed, but I couldn't help thinking that the old Maroons must have been quite a team to wear such big uniforms.

Saturday came too soon and we went to Melvindale for the game. They have quite a plant there—a beautiful field and good dressing facilities—and all of a sudden I found the idea of going out onto the field in our 1911 model uniforms almost as great a challenge than I could handle.

We sat around the dressing room saying nothing until someone shouted that it was our turn to warm up. Everybody just sat for a minute. Finally Lyle got up and started for the door and the rest of us followed. No one busted the door the way we should have, no one cared if he lived long enough to reach the field. But, almost automatically, we hit the gridiron and started charging up and down the field in short spurts. At first the crowd seemed to be cheering our amazing costumes, but in a short time we became aware that they were laughing at us.

I heard one guy yell, "If you're for real, I'm glad I'm a fake." They started calling us the Toledo Antiques, and even the referee came over and asked if these were the uniforms we were going to play in. It couldn't have been worse if we'd gone out there naked.

It didn't help any when the Melvindale team showed up dressed in sharp new green and white uniforms with shiny white plastic helmets and pants that fit them like bikinis.

The first half was a nightmare. I played quarterback on offense, but don't ask me what I was calling. Our helmets would not stay on right, the pants were too loose, and we couldn't do anything right. We were blocking into our own ball carriers, falling over ourselves, and moving around in a semi—daze. Normally, I'd have all kinds of trouble keeping the guys quiet in the huddle. They'd all be telling me to run the play over them, or to let them carry or to hit them with a pass. That's one of the quarterback's problems. Each guy is so sure that he can blast his man easily and he's trying to call the game for you.

This night, however, all the conversation was about the uniforms. We couldn't run. We couldn't hit. The halftime score was 14-0 and we were lucky it wasn't worse.

Frankly, I didn't care anything about the score. All I wanted to do was get the game over with, get out of the uniform, and go hide. I wasn't tired; I wasn't hot. I was just plain miserable—sick of being laughed at, sick of everything, sick of everybody.

It was crazy. Nobody had injuries. Nobody had anything to say. Nobody even got up to get a drink. We just sat. Finally Lyle went out and came back with the old man. He was as low as the rest of us.

"He's been taking a lot of abuse from those clowns in the stands," Lyle explained. "Who do the son-of-bitches think they are?"

It was just then that a chill hit me. I raised my head and looked around. The other guys were starting to straighten up, too. It was like an awakening. Someone yelled, "Let's get out there gang!" It might have been me. I don't know. I don't remember too well everything that I did after that.

We hit the door and kept blasting through. The band hadn't finished its number, but we shot out among them yelling and charging.

"It's our field," Lyle or someone yelled. "Nobody allowed on our field."

The band hustled off, frightened, and we were really high. Let'em laugh, but they'd be laughing with their faces in the mud. We were crazy, It was all unreal.

Suddenly I could see everything. I could sense things before they happened. Our line wasn't opening holes, it was pushing their line back. I could call anything and it worked like magic. It was a one-team show. I shouted all through the game; and when it ended we won, 28-14. I don't remember if I was laughing or crying. I do know that by the time we stalked proudly off the field, a lot of the crowd was cheering for us. As soon as I reached the dressing room it all left me.

Suddenly I was more sore and more tired than I'd ever been after a game. I managed to get out of the uniform and into a shower. When I returned my uniform and the others were gone. The old man must had collected them and put them in several car trunks, but I really don't know.

We had a good payday from the game and Monday we were able to get credit from the Athletic Supply for new uniforms.

In the excitement of the season, I didn't give the old guy any more thought, but one night I asked Lyle how he was doing.

"How would I know?" Lyle shot back. "I haven't seen him since the game. How did you ever come up with him?"

"I never saw him before he offered those uniforms," I assured him. Neither of us, it turned out, even knew his name.

Well, we never got around to looking him up. I don't know if he's still around. Probably not. But if I weren't a cop, I'd wonder whether that was us playing in those uniforms that second half or if that was the last game for the great old Toledo Maroons.

CHAPTER 39
SUICIDE OR HOMICIDE

Shedding the uniform and becoming a detective. The big day that every uniform officer dreams of. I kept reading the order over to make sure it was true.

What a strange feeling going to work and not wearing the uniform. It will be nice not being so conspicuous. In uniform I had the feeling everyone was staring at me. I was in the spot light. A few of my friends at the station smiled and made remarks when they saw me in plain-clothes. I felt a little awkward seeing them in their uniforms and me out of mine.

Captain Arnold, head of Homicide, was standing in the doorway to his office and motioned for me to come into his office. He sat behind his desk and pointed to a chair. He welcomed me to his unit. "Bob, we're glad to have you. You probably already know you're replacing Detective Cartledge. He's retiring next month. We're going to miss him. I think he's the best detective we ever had. You're lucky he's going to train you. You pay attention to him and you'll learn a lot."

"Yes Sir, I seen Detective Cartledge in action over the years. I have a lot of respect for him. I hope I can be half as good."

Detective Cartledge was sitting at his desk talking on the phone. I walked up to him. He squinted and nodded for me to take a chair close by. I smiled when I saw a miniature electric chair on his desk with the caption written on it. "Plug it in."

He put the phone down and looked directly at me. "You're the new guy?" He stood up and extended his hand and we shook.

"I'm glad to meet you." I begun to explain how nice it was going to be working with him. He cut me short, got up and put his coat on.

"Let's go, we got a dead one. Skip the bullshit."

He drove and didn't say a word. From the expression on his face he was probably thinking of the information he received over the phone concerning the case. He parked in front of a nice home where yellow crime scene tape circled the yard. Detective Cartledge lifted the tape and we ducked under and walked to where two uniformed officers and a sergeant were standing.

He looked directly in the sergeant's eyes. "Did anybody taint the scene?"

"No, Sir. We went into the home and saw the man and determined he was dead for some time. We immediately exited and protected the home so no one could enter."

"Very good sergeant, thanks."

Detective Cartledge walked around the outside of the house. He examined every window and door. He stopped and looked at me. "Did you notice anything?"

"Yes, none of the windows or doors show any sign of forced entry."

"Good, now lets go inside." He took off his shoes and I did the same. As soon as we entered he stooped and examined the shiny floor for shoe prints. He walked slowly inside looking for drawers, or cupboards left open. The whole home was clean and nothing seemed out of order. We walked into the den where the body was. Detective Cartledge studied the whole room before approaching the deceased man. A white male about sixty years old was slouched in a chair with his arms dangling over the arm rests. His head was leaning to the left in an awkward position. His right temple had a wound that appeared to be made from a gun shot. A small sliver of dried blood was below the wound.

Detective Cartledge stood over the body. He pointed to the wound. "Tell me, what does that tell you?"

"It tells me that the caliber was from a small hand gun. It

was fired close to the head since there are powder burns on the skin. Tattooing is all around the wound."

"That's good. What do you think of the overall scene? Is it a homicide or a suicide?"

"Everything I see indicates suicide. There was no forced entry. No cabinets were left open. Nothing appears to have been taken. No signs of a struggle, the man's clothing are not torn, or roughed up. There are no bruises on his body. One thing bothers me. If this man committed suicide by shooting, where is the gun?"

"Good thinking. The problem is finding the gun. If we find the gun we solve the case. If this man shot himself the gun has to be in this room." He stood thinking, then said. "Bob, I want you to go over every inch of this room. Somewhere in here is the answer."

We didn't talk anymore. He concentrated on the left side of the room and I took the right. After about fifteen minutes he said, "Bob, you see anything that might shed some light on this case?"

"Yes, why is the chair with the body so close to the fireplace?"

"I was thinking the same thing. Come here by the fireplace, I want to show you something. He pointed into the ashes. "You see that chip of brick? It was recently broken off." I saw the chip but couldn't relate it to the dead man. I shook my head like I didn't understand.

"I'm sorry Ben, it don't make any sense to me."

He kept staring at the chip, then looked at me. "Bob, get on your back and shine your flashlight up that chimney." I did what he said and I couldn't believe what I saw. The hairs on the back of my neck bristled. I shouted. "Hey, there's a gun hanging up there. It's a stainless steel thirty eight snub nosed revolver. It's hooked to a large rubber band." I reached up and got it.

We examined the revolver. There were five live rounds and one spent in the cylinder. Detective Cartledge pointed at the spent shell. "That's the one that got him." The gun was carefully protected for prints to be sent to the lab for further examination.

Detective Cartledge reconstructed what had happened. "The man wanted to take his life. He knew if he committed suicide his insurance wouldn't pay. There's probably a clause in his policy that states if you commit suicide they will void it. He wanted to protect his family so they could get the money. He set this up so it would look like he was murdered. He secured the large rubber band in the chimney then attached the gun to it. He pushed the chair close to the fireplace so he could stretch the rubber band to his head. When he shot himself the rubber band snapped the gun up the chimney out of sight. When the gun was traveling up the chimney it made contact with a brick chipping it."

I stared at him with amazement. He patted me on the back and said. "Well, you solved your first case. Type up the report."

CHAPTER 40
AN INCIDENT TO REMEMBER

"Unit One, this is the dispatcher. Summit and Cherry at the High Way Bar, disturbance a man with a gun."

"Unit One, okay." My partner Jim was driving. He activated the red lights and pushed his foot down on the gas pedal. The speed forced us back in our seats. The bright lights in front of the many cafes along skid row took on the appearance of a multi-colored blur due to the speed of the scout car.

A large heavy-set woman was standing in the street flailing her arms. Jim pulled the car to the curb and no sooner stopped when the woman forced the upper part of her huge body into the window next to me. I slid to the middle of the seat and stared at her. Her face flushed, red with small streams of perspiration running down her cheeks. The arm bands on her short sleeved dress were digging into her large arms. A tattoo of an eagle on her right forearm had "Love Harry" drawn under it. Out of breath she gasped for air as she shouted, "Willie the wine-head is inside with a machine gun. He means business. He ran me and my customers out. I never saw him act like this. The man's crazy."

I motioned for her to get her head out of the window so I could get out. She couldn't, she had jammed her body in the window and was stuck. She jerked hard and her head hit the ceiling. She let out a barrage of cuss words. My partner and I both exited the car from the driver's side. We got behind the huge woman and grabbed her by the waist and pulled her from the window. She rubbed her head a couple of times and pointed to the door of the bar. "He's in there. You better watch yourselves."

Jim nodded, "Okay, lady, wait for us by our car."

We tried to look in the front window of the bar but the blinds were closed. Jim slowly opened the door a crack and peeked in. "Bob, he's at the back sitting at a table. He's facing this door. He knows we're here and he's going to see us enter. Be ready for anything." We both drew our guns and carefully opened the door. The guy glared at us. He was a small thin man wearing a dirty white shirt with the sleeves rolled up. His hands were inside a violin case. The only noise was a large fan straining to make a breeze. We separated in case he started shooting.

Jim said in a soft tone. "Willie, you keep your hands inside that case. Don't do any thing crazy." The man's eyes widen and he started laughing. We both pointed our guns at him and continued to slowly walk to him. The man kept laughing but we kept edging closer. When we were about five feet away from him we both must've of had the same idea. We dove and pushed down on the cover of the violin case clamping his hands inside. Willie screamed but we kept the pressure on until we grabbed his wrists and pulled his hands from the case. Inside was dirty socks, undershorts, and soiled tee shirts.

Jim slid the violin case away from Willie and pointed at him. "What's going on here?"

Willie laughed nervously. "You see that big water buffalo that's standing by your car? She's been beating me up for years. The other day I took my last one and was thinking of a way to get even with her. I was walking past Stein's pawn shop and saw this violin case in the window. I paid fifty cents for it and came in here and all I did was put my hands inside of it and laugh. Man, you should of seen that woman move her three hundred and fifty pounds. I never laughed so hard in all my life. I would of paid five-thousand dollars for that violin case to see that show. "

The laughter evaporated when Willie saw the big woman

standing behind us with her hands on her hips. She shouted. "Officers, there's no need to take him to jail. I'll take care of him."

Willie jumped up and grabbed my arm. "Officer, I did wrong. It's your duty to take me to jail. If you're not going to jail me, carry me a couple blocks away from here. I promise I won't come back."

We motioned for Willie to follow us. We were going to make our decision in the scout car away from the woman. Willie followed but he kept looking over his shoulder to see where she was. I turned and saw her fist clenched and she was pointing at him. Seeing me, she quickly unraveled her fist and started waving and forced a smile.

We opened the back door of the scout car and motioned for Willie to get in. He bent and was almost inside when he came flying back out and landed on the sidewalk. A loud voice from inside, "This cab is already taken."

We were startled and looked inside. A man was sitting on the back seat. He yelled at us. "Take me to Adams and Franklin and step it up, or I won't give you a tip."

From the sound of his voice we could tell he was intoxicated. I pointed at him and said.

"Listen you. This is not a cab. It's a police car. Get out!"

"Hey, I never had trouble with the Black and White cabs before. What are you, a wise guy?"

We tried to explain but he was too drunk. He looked down at Willie. "I'm not going to share my cab with a wine-head."

Willie shook his head. "Man, that guy ain't drunk. He's crazy talking like that."

Jim reached down and lifted Willie to his feet. "You okay?"

"Yeah, I'm alright."

"How far from this bar will you be if we turn you loose?"

Willie's face lit up. "Very." He handed me the violin case and said, "You take it. It served its purpose." He looked at the door of the bar to make sure the big woman wasn't there then took off running like a track star..

The guy in the back seat became impatient and started crawling out of the car challenging us to a fight. We informed him we would not only give him a ride, we'd get him accommodations for the night. He enjoyed the ride but turned hostile when he saw his sleeping quarters.

CHAPTER 41
I AIN'T DOING THAT AGAIN

Harold Hinkle, the practical joker, drained the last of the gun powder from a large firecracker. He laughed so hard thinking about what he was going to do with it, he could hardly put the fuse back in the hole. He walked to the neighborhood tavern, smiling and rubbing the powderless firecracker hidden in his pocket.

His friends were crowded around the bar talking sports. Harold got a beer and joined in. He slowly took the firecracker out and put it on a saucer. All conversation stopped while the guys stared at the large firecracker. Harold took his lighter and lit the fuse. The fuse smoldered and spit sparks. The men couldn't believe what Harold did. They just stood there. Harold picked up a glass and put it over the lit firecracker. Someone yelled, "Are you crazy? That glass will blind you." Everyone ducked for cover under tables. Harold just sat there smiling watching the fuse burn down.

The men slowly got up from the floor. One guy pointed at Harold, "You ever pull a stunt like that again I'll kick hell out of you."

A few days later Harold watched the men at the shop go to the water cooler and get a drink. The owner of the place purchased water in five gallon bottles. He was a clean freak and scared of what might be in the city water. The following day Harold brought in four goldfish. When nobody was looking he quickly turned the large bottle upside down and dropped the fish inside. A short time later, a mechanic pulled a paper cup from the dispenser and was getting ready to draw water. When he saw the fish swimming his head shot back. "Damn, there's critters in the water." From then on every time someone went for a drink they examined the inside of the bottle.

There was a guy in the shop named McSevich who was mean and everyone steered clear of him. Whenever McSevich worked the midnight shift he would constantly complain because he couldn't get to sleep in the daytime. Harold heard McSevich yell, "I get home at seven and I lay awake until eleven before I fall asleep. Humans are meant to sleep at night." His bitching kept up all through the shift.

Harold laughed. The next morning he went to the newspaper and talked to the clerk in the classified section. He told her his name was McSevich and gave her McSevich's address and phone number. He then placed a for sale ad that read, *Brand new Ford Fairlane Five Hundred. Only seven hundred miles. I got drafted into the Army and must sell fast. Price Five hundred dollars. Please call between the hours of 11:00 am and 1:00 pm.*

The clerk squinted, "Mr. McSevich, are you sure you only want five hundred dollars for that car? That's awful cheap."

"Yes, I'm in a bind and I have to get rid of it."

The day after the ad appeared in the paper McSevich came to work with bloodshot eyes, cussing. He shouted how his phone rang off the hook and the fools on the other end wouldn't listen to him. He had to threaten a few of them to get them off the line. He called the paper and gave them a piece of his mind. They told him this never happened before. He said it better not ever happen to him again. Harold had to go to another room he was laughing so hard.

After work, most of the guys stopped at the neighborhood bar. Before Harold went to the bar he had to go to a department store to pick up a few things. When he was walking down the aisle he passed the cosmetics counter. He stopped and smiled. He bought a bottle of cheap perfume that had a sprayer. He put the bottle in his pocket and went to the tavern. The guys were all sitting on stools at the bar. He secretly took the bottle of perfume from his pocket and walked past them and sprayed their backs. He than sat at the end of the bar and laughed when he saw them sniffing. One of them said. "Man, it smells like a French cathouse in here." Needless to say there were a lot of hostile wives when the men got home.

At work, the guys exchanged stories of what happened when their wives smelled the perfume. Harold got the biggest kick out of that. He thought the perfume spraying deserved another shot. Again the guys stopped after work and were sitting at the bar. Harold took out the perfume bottle and started spraying their backs. One guy spun around on the bar stool and his elbow struck the perfume bottle knocking it to the floor. His eyes widened and he grabbed Harold by the throat. "So you're the bastard." They all jumped from their stools and got their licks on Harold.

We were dispatched to the hospital. Harold was all bandaged up. We asked him what happened. He just shook his head. "Never mind officers. I'll never pull that stunt again."

CHAPTER 42
THE FIGHTING HIBISCUS

Being a city boy and a police officer for thirty-three years I never learned much about plants. Oh yeah, I cut the grass but that was about it. I retired and came to Florida and had a home built by a contractor and he put in the sod. He explained I would have to plant the trees and flowers. I went to Home Depot and filled a large cart with young trees and plants. I came home and dug holes and dropped the trees and plants in. I filled the remaining hole with dirt, then stamped the loose soil with my shoes. I walked away slapping the dirt from my hands and felt pretty good.

I was under the impression that all one had to do is put the plants and trees into the ground and they take care of themselves. In a few days I found out I was wrong. I noticed one of the Hibiscus plants was losing its leaves. It was much smaller then the other Hibiscus planted the same day. I didn't pay much attention to the plant until I saw a rabbit eating it. I chased it away then examined the stunted plant and saw there were caterpillars on it. On the stems were a lot of small bugs that I later learned were aphids. Being a city boy I didn't realize what was happening and felt if the plant died I would just buy another one.

A couple days later a powerful storm hit the area. High winds flung a large limb onto the small Hibiscus. The storm passed and I went into the yard and lifted the large limb. The small plant was smashed into the ground. Most of its limbs were broken or cracked. I reached down to pull it up and pitch it into the garbage can when I saw the most beautiful flower I have ever seen blooming from one of the crushed branches. I straightened up and stared at this pitiful sight. Here was a plant that was attacked by rabbits, caterpillars, aphids and crushed by a huge limb and it still managed to smile by growing a beautiful flower. As I stood there my life flashed by and I thought, how many times I was beat down and yet I managed to fight back and come out a winner. I took my bumps and yet I always managed to smile. I ran into the house and got some tongue depressors and small strips of white cloth. Every thin stem on this small Hibiscus that was cracked, or broken I put a splint on. I braced a stick under this small warrior so it could stand and be proud.

My neighbor came over and stared at me. "What the hell you doing growing a rag plant?" I tried to explain to him I was going to save the plant's life. He didn't understand. He laughed and said. "Throw the damn thing away and get another one."

I didn't try to explain any more. I drove back to Home Depot and told the salesman in the garden section that I wanted to save this plant. He squinted and shook his head. "Sir, it would be cheaper to purchase a new plant." While he was still talking, I went to the shelves where the bug sprays were and read every label on the cans until I found the one that I thought would kill the caterpillars. I did the same thing to pick out the poison that would take care of the aphids. I bought a large section of fence that I could put around the little fighting Hibiscus so the rabbits couldn't get their mouths on its leaves. I got a hose and a special nozzle, then went to the fertilizer section and again read every label on the bags. When I thought, I had the right one for my Hibiscus I bought two bags. On the way home I stopped at the library and got three books on plants.

I pulled in my driveway and was unloading all the things I bought to save my proud plant into my new wheelbarrow. I turned around and there stood my neighbor with his arms crossed and shaking his head. "A hundred dollars worth of stuff to save a five-dollar plant. Man, I don't understand your logic."

"Well, I understand my logic and that's all that matters." I ignored him and pushed the wheelbarrow next to the fighting Hibiscus and dropped to my knees and went to work.

Every day I look into my back yard. The other plants are all much bigger and full of flowers but I don't pay attention to them. I examine my little fighter and offer it words of encouragement. I loosen the soil around it with my hands. When the small limbs mended, I removed the splints.

If I have a bad day and feel my problems are mounting I walk to the back yard and look down at that little Hibiscus and smile. It responded last week by opening three new flowers. I believe it's trying to tell me something. You bet I'm listening.

CHAPTER 43
TWO BANGED UP JOBS

Carlos stepped out of the cab, wearing his prison issue pin-striped suit. He had served ten years and this was his first day back in the old neighborhood. When his friends greeted him, they looked at his clothes and smirked. He thought, in no time at all they'd have a different outlook. He walked to his friend's home and knocked on the door. John answered and immediately shook his friend's hand. "Man. Carlos it's been a long time. I'm glad to see you."

They talked a little and Carlos got serious. "You want to make some real money, John?"

"My ears are always open for that type of talk."

"Have you blown any safes lately?"

"Nah. Man. It's almost impossible to get dynamite. Forget about buying it, if you got a record. I used to be able to steal it at the quarry, but they shut that down."

"In the can one of the cons serving a long term told me where he hid some nitro. Have you ever worked with nitroglycerin?"

"No, but I don't think it would be much different from dynamite. I know you can't rough the stuff, or it will go off."

"Are you in? The nitro is hid in the abandoned factory on Michigan Street. Let's go there after dark tonight."

"I'm with you. I'll pick you up at eleven."

John parked his car a block away from the factory. Carlos put a crow bar under his coat. They walked on the sidewalk and when they were sure no one was looking they dashed to the factory. Sturdy boards were nailed across the door.

Carlos quickly took the crowbar and began prying the boards away. Once inside he led the way with a flashlight. Both men waved the cobwebs away from their faces. Every once in a while a rat scurried across the floor.

"Listen, John, the guy said he hid the stuff in a small storage room inside the large area with the punch presses." He moved the beam of the flashlight until he saw a door marked storage. "That must be it." He quickly went to it and pried the lock with the crowbar. A screeching sound and the lock broke free of the latch. He pointed the light inside. Two gallon jugs of clear liquid were in the corner on the floor. Carlos started to run inside.

John put out his arm, blocking him. "Hold it man, move that stuff too quick and we won't be here long. You gotta to be gentle with nitro. You carry one jug and I'll take the other one. That way they won't bang together and explode." They tenderly lifted the jugs and walked softly on their tiptoes out of the factory.

When they got to the car, John opened the back door. "Let's put these jugs on the floor. You put yours on that side and I'll put mine on this side. The ride is smoother in the back seat area."

"Where are we going to store this stuff tonight, John?"

"Hell, lets use it tonight. I know where there's a furniture store with a lot of money in the safe. I've been casing the place for a year. Let's knock it over tonight. I carry my tools in the trunk."

They parked the car in a dark area of the furniture store parking lot. John carried his tools and Carlos carried one of the jugs of nitroglycerine. John smashed a window and pulled all the splintered glass from the frame. Carlos asked. "Why you pulling all those pieces of glass out?"

"So the cops won't see them if they shine their lights on the window." They both crawled inside and went to the large safe. John drilled holes in it, then put soap in the lower ones. He put a funnel in one of the upper holes. He motioned for Carlos to give him the nitro.

He carefully poured the liquid into the funnel and the nitro drained inside the safe. He handed the jug and funnel back to Carlos. "We'll take this jug with the remaining nitro to another room. I don't want it to explode when this safe blows." They went to the other room and left the jug and funnel. John pointed to a mattress. "Help me carry it back to the safe."

"What you going to do with that mattress?"

"We're going to hold it against the safe so when it explodes this will muffle the sound."

"Hey, John, you think of everything. You know your stuff."

"Damn straight." John reached into his bag and took out a detonator and three feet of wick. He pushed the detonator into the top hole of the safe and forced it down until it made contact with the nitro. "Now, all we gotta do is light the wick and push the mattress as hard as we can against the safe door."

"No, John, We got one more thing to do. Take all the money in this safe when it blows and get the hell out of here."

John laughed and lit the wick, It sputtered sparks until it went inside the safe, then smoke came out the holes. A powerful explosion shook the building.

The next morning when the manager unlocked the front door and went inside, he immediately smelled a strong odor. He noticed the gallon jug with clear liquid on the floor.

He ran to the room where the safe was. His eyes widened when he saw the front of the safe blown off and two men stuck to the wall with the safe door and mattress sticking in them. He ran to the phone in the other office and called the police.

The first crew responded and the manager met them outside screaming and pointing to the door. He ran inside to the safe and the officers chased after him. The officers' eyes widened when they saw the two dead burglars. One of them said. "They won't have the guts to do that again."

The other one nodded. "We'll need a spatula to get them off that wall."

After the manager calmed down, he took them to the jug

with the remaining   nitroglycerine in the other room. Searching the parking lot, the burglars' car was found with the other jug of nitro.

The bomb squad was called and Lieutenant Sinclair responded. The lieutenant was known for not being afraid of bombs no matter how big they were. Most guys had a different take on why he wasn't scared. They said, Sinclair himself was bombed most of the time. He came in the furniture store and walked to the room where the safe was blown. He glanced at the two guys pinned on the wall and didn't say anything. He shouted, "Where the hell is the nitro?" A patrolman pointed to the jug. Lieutenant Sinclair didn't hesitate. He walked over and grabbed it. Everyone in the room flinched as the liquid swished inside.

He carried the jug to the burglars' car where a patrolman pointed to the floor of the backseat. The lieutenant yanked open the door and snatched the full jug of nitroglycerine. Both jugs struck each other. Everyone cringed. Lieutenant Sinclair now was carrying the two jugs to his car. The jugs clinked together a couple more times. Everyone backed up and stayed as far away from him as possible. He put the nitro in his car and drove off.

The officers breathed easier. One of them said, "Glad to see him leave. One day that fool is going to kill himself handling that stuff."

Another one said. "I don't want to be around when he does."

Lieutenant Sinclair drove to a public park about a half mile away. He evacuated everyone from the area.   A bulldozer was brought to the park on a trailer. It scraped a hole about six feet deep. Lieutenant Sinclair took a shovel and in the center dug a smaller hole and placed the two gallon jugs of nitro in it. He placed a detonator and about thirty-five feet of fuse to the jugs than shoveled dirt on top of them. He ordered three truck loads of sand for screening to be put over the jugs. The trucks showed up but they didn't have sand. They were loaded with small stones. The lieutenant didn't seem to care. He directed the trucks to unload the stones in the hole the bulldozer had scraped. He didn't tell the truck drivers what they were dropping the stones on.

When the hole was completely filled the trucks left. Lieutenant Sinclair didn't hesitate. He lit the fuse and watched the flashing sparks run down the wick and under the stones. He ran to a large tree and got behind it.

A gigantic explosion sent shock waves and stones in every direction. Windows were being broken a mile away. People dove for cover. The police switchboard lit up like a pinball machine. Police cars with sirens wailing and red lights flashing raced to the park.

When they arrived, Lieutenant Sinclair was getting up from the ground covered with white dust. The uniformed officers asked him what happened. He mumbled a few cuss words and walked to his car that had hundreds of dents and the windows blown out. He drove off.

The officers stood there looking at the large crater and stones strewed all over the place.

CHAPTER 44
WELCOME BACK

My partner and I were going over robbery reports of convenience stores from the past week. We had a good idea who was responsible, because the perpetrator was using the same M.O. The description of the man was identical in all the robberies. Dick looked at me. "Sure as hell this has to be Leon Mitchell doing this." I nodded.

"Bob, Leon is one slick customer. He doesn't stay at one address long. I remember the last time we were after him, we had a devil of a time finding him."

Did you check to see if he might be in jail now? What's the use of looking for him if he was in jail when these robberies went down?"

"Man, that's the first thing I did. He's been out for a year."

We continued talking and mapping out strategy on how to find Leon Mitchell when a uniform unit came over the police radio. They must have been thinking the same thing we were. "Unit seven to the detective bureau. We have one Leon Mitchell. He is wanted on minor warrants. Would any detective like to talk with him about other incidents, before we book him?"

Dick and I jumped almost knocking each other down rushing for the microphone on the reception desk. I managed to grab it and pushed the button. "Bring him to the detective bureau. We definitely are interested in this subject."

"Unit seven, we're on our way."

Dick always had a sense of humor. He was busy making a

sign with a marker pen. It read, **WELCOME BACK LEON. WE MISSED YOU.** He got some scotch tape and stuck it over the door to the prisoner holding room. We both stood back and laughed.

In about twenty-five minutes two uniformed officers led handcuffed Leon Mitchell into the detective bureau. As soon as he saw the sign he smiled, "Ain't this a bitch."

I uncuffed him and pointed to a desk by a window. "Come on Leon, you're one of our favorite customers. We don't need to go into that stuffy holding room. Let's sit by the window and talk." Leon, Dick and I sat at the desk.

Leon looked at me. "Man, what's this bullshit about? I ain't done nothing."

I smiled at him. "You know the game. Before I can answer that, I gotta read you your rights."

"Man. You don't need to read me my rights." He than recited the rights from memory and didn't miss a word. "I heard that bullshit so many times it's boring."

"That's great, Leon, you haven't lost your touch. I'm glad you know we always start out that way. I can see it in your eyes you're looking for a deal. I'll give you some slack like we always do. Here's what we got to offer. We know you did ten robberies. You tell us about them and we'll drop a few. You know our word is gold."

"Aw man, that judge is going to hang my ass."

"It always looks bad at this stage of the game. How many times did you go to court and came out smelling like a rose? Our main concern right now is stopping these robberies before somebody gets hurt or killed. You were lucky a couple times, the owners of the places had guns but couldn't get to them. I guarantee the next time you go in their places with your hand in your pocket pretending you have a gun, they'll shoot you."

Leon slowly nodded his head. Dick and I thought he was ready to talk. Instead, he blurted out. "Man. I want to see my attorney."

Dick asked. "Is Bricker, still your lawyer?"

"Yeah, man. I don't want to talk until he tells me to."

Attorney James Bricker handled most cases involving hardened criminals. When we went to court and knew he was defending the accused, we knew we were going to get grilled on the stand. I was looking out the window and there was Attorney Bricker walking from the Municipal Court Building to the State Court Building. I pointed at him. Leon leaned forward and saw him. I got up and told him I'd be right back then quickly took the steps downstairs and out the door. I shouted at the attorney. He turned around and waited for me to catch up to him. He smiled, "What's your problem, Detective?"

"Well, I got Leon Mitchell in my office. I believe he's responsible for a lot of robberies. He says he doesn't want to talk until you tell him."

Attorney Bricker eyes' widened and he shrugged his shoulders. "Talk to him all you want. He doesn't have any money on my desk."

I went back to the office. I asked Leon if he saw me talking to the attorney. He nodded.

"Well, your attorney said I could talk with you." Leon then confessed to the robberies.

*　　*　　*　　*

Two months later we went to court to testify to what Leon Mitchell told us. Attorney Bricker had a mean look, like he couldn't wait to question and tear me apart.

I took the stand. He got up from the table where Leon Mitchell was sitting next to him.

He walked in front of me and pointed. "Are you aware that you violated my client's rights?"

"No, Sir, I didn't violate Mister Mitchell's rights."

"Mister Mitchell, asked for his attorney and you denied him."

"No, Sir. Remember when I ran up to you on the sidewalk between the court buildings and you said there's no mon......

He looked shocked and started stuttering. **"Never mind. Ignore that question."**

CHAPTER 45
LITTLE CON

All the boys in the neighborhood liked to play cowboys and Indians, cops and robbers, and soldiers — That is, all except Marty Carle. He was eleven years old and his idol was Al Capone. Marty dressed just like Capone. He wore a brown double breasted pin-striped suit, pointed shoes, necktie and a Fedora hat with a wide brim that was pulled down over his left eye.

The other boys asked Marty to join in the games they were playing. Marty would shake his head, frown and yell out, "Cowboys smell like horseshit. Indians run around naked and freeze their asses off in the winter. Soldiers get shot. That stuff is not for me. I want to be a con-man and make a lot of money. Look at the cons and the pimps around here. They all got nice clothes and fancy cars. That's what I want."

It didn't take long for Marty to pick up the nickname Little Con. One of his first endeavors was operating a penny-pitching game. People would throw pennies against a building and whoever came closest to the wall won. Little Con would pick up all the pennies and take a percentage of them and the remaining pennies went to the winner.

Every place little Con went, a deck of cards went with him. If he saw a group of boys hanging around and he knew they had money, a card game would surely start. He liked to hang around the station where the newsboys got their papers. It seemed the newsboys always had money. The school bus was another good place for his card games. The kids on the bus all had lunch money and a lot of them went hungry after the games. The guy who ran the poolroom hired Little Con to pass out football betting sheets to the homes in the area. The cops never suspected an eleven-year old would be mixed up with gambling. I lived a couple houses from him. I always liked him but I never let myself get caught up in his schemes. As we got older we went our separate ways. I joined the police department and Little Con continued his scams. I thought it funny that nobody got wise to him. I do believe, if ever he decided to become an honest salesman, he could make a lot of money.

When he was old enough to go into bars he used this ruse. He and his buddy would walk into the bar. Little Con pretended he was drunk. He put his head on a table and faked he was sleeping. His buddy would take bets that Little Con would not raise his head until the bar closed. Sometimes he'd keep his head down for two hours. When the bartender shouted the bar was closing Little Con would jump up, run to his buddy and they would split the money.

One day when I was working we answered a call where a guy set a Gypsy fortune-telling place on fire. This was not unusual since a lot of men were lured into this place and rolled of their money. We had a lot of complaints but no one would make a formal one. The Gypsies scam worked this way. A good-looking woman sat in front of a large window. She waved at the men walking by and made gestures like she was a prostitute. Once inside two other women joined the one who was in the window. They would dance and rub their hands on the guy. One of them would remove his wallet. The guy would start to yell and the Gypsy men would come from behind a curtain and throw him out.

This date when we pulled up the firemen had extinguished the blaze. The Gypsies were all out on the sidewalk yelling. There were so many of them it reminded me of an ant hill that had been disturbed. I asked one of the men what happened. He pointed to a large hole in the bay window. He said, "A convertible stopped in front of his business and a guy dressed in a brown suit stood up in the back seat and he had a bow and arrow with a rag on the arrow. He set the rag on fire and shot it through the bay window where it stuck in the curtain setting the place on fire."

I asked him why the guy did this and what kind of car he was in.

He shrugged his shoulders and said, "I don't know why he did it. He was a passenger in a big new powder-blue Cadillac." He couldn't describe the driver.

We went inside and I saw what was left of the arrow. In the corner I noticed a brown dress hat with a large brim. I looked at the guy. "Did you people give this guy a Gypsy-good time. Is that why he shot that arrow?"

He watched me looking at the brown hat on the floor and figured I knew something and he'd better be careful how he answered me. He stuttered and I stared into his eyes. "I want the truth. We don't want to put a lot of work on this case and you're lying. Do you understand? If you're lying we'll arrest you for making out a false police report."

He just stood there then said, "I don't want to make a report."

The next day I drove through the old neighborhood. I saw Little Con washing his powder-blue Caddy. I parked and walked up to him. He put out his hand and we shook. "Wow, Bob, great seeing you."

"Same here how's it going? I don't see you wearing your hat with the large brim,"

He looked serious. "Why you say that for?"

I smiled and looked in the back seat of his car and saw the bow. I pointed at it. "What did you do change your mind? I thought Indians freeze their asses off running around naked."

"Aw, Bob, what's the gig? Man, I don't know what your getting at."

I started laughing. "You must be hard up playing around with those Gypsy broads. Tell me is that Gypsy-good-time any good?"

"Hey man! Let's get something straight. I wasn't looking for a broad when I went in. I was watching all those suckers going in there getting fleeced. I figured the Gypsies had a lot of dough ripping off those idiots. I wanted to put a little hustle on them and make a few bucks. I went inside and right away these broads started dancing and jumping all around me. They grabbed my balls a couple of times and I knew something was going on. I felt for my wallet and it was gone. Man, I started raising hell and a bunch of guys threw me out. I went back and got even."

"Well, if you want your hat, it's still in the place. It has some charred marks on it."

"Nah, I'm done with those thieves."

"It was good talking to you, Little Con. See you around." I started to walk back to my car.

"Hey, Bob, I got a good deal for you. How much do you make a month being a cop?"

"I do all right. Why?"

"Get with me on this and you'll make more money in one night than you do in a month."

"No thanks. What are you going to do, start up a Gypsy-good-time joint?"

"Aw, man, forget it."

I didn't see Little Con for a few years. My new district was on the outskirts of the city. This area was sparsely populated. A funeral home was surrounded by farm fields. My partner and I noticed a lot of cars parked all night in the funeral home parking lot almost every weekend. We thought it strange all those cars parked and no lights on. Then I saw the powder-blue Cadillac parked right by the back door. I figured out what was going on now.

One night the dispatcher sent us to the funeral home. He said, "Assist the Rescue Squad and let us know what is going on." When we arrived my partner and I jumped from the car and ran to the side door. There was only one car in the parking lot --- a powder-blue Cadillac. The other cars had high tailed it out of there. We heard voices in the basement. I went down the steps and there stood Little Con looking up at me.

"Oh, Bob, am I glad to see you."

"What did you get yourself into now?"

"Aw, this is crazy. Some damn drunken broad got into one of those caskets and this other stupid broad closed the lid and it locked. We tried to get her out but the lid wouldn't budge. I thought she might suffocate so I called the Rescue Squad."

The guys from the Rescue Squad pried open the casket and a naked girl jumped out screaming, "I want out of this creepy place." She pointed at Little Con, "That man is crazy. Playing cards in a damn funeral home."

I took her to another room and talked with her. She said, Little Con hired her and another girl to walk around naked while the card games were going on. They would distract the players and when they turned their heads and looked at us, Little Con would stack the deck.

When I came out of the room I told Little Con what the girl said. He shrugged his shoulders and his hands went out from his sides. "Bob, look around does this look like a gambling joint? Man, who you going to believe a dumb broad whose brain is screwed up by being deprived of air, or me, a upstanding friend. Bob you've known me for a long time."

"Yeah, I sure do."

CHAPTER 46
BISHOP

The radio came alive. "Unit 10 - Robbery in progress, step it up sounds serious." This was the day I met Bishop. With red lights flashing and siren wailing, we pulled up to the scene. My eyes widened when I saw a huge woman sitting on the chest of a guy sprawled out on the ground. Every time he said something she'd whack him in the head with a Bible and yell.

"Hush that hole in your face rogue, cause the only thing that comes out is lies." We exited the car and ran to them. The guy pleaded for us to get her off. My partner and I grabbed an arm and pulled her up. She was an older woman, stood at least six-foot three and must have weighed three hundred pounds. We warned the guy on the ground, "Stay put."

She yelled, "Sucker, you best stay where you're at, or I'll pound your sorry ass into tomorrow."

We asked her what happened. She pointed at the guy. "This thievin' mother-fucker tried to snatch my purse. I know these no-goods in this neighborhood are always looking for an easy take. This fool learned his lesson. You see, I always carry my purse in my left hand. That leaves my right hand free to pop the dummy who grabs it. The sorry son-of-a-bitch grabbed and I smashed him right between his eyes. He dropped like a bag of garbage. I jumped on the fool til you came." She looked down at the guy. "Ain't that right, thug?"

He didn't look up and he didn't say anything. She slammed him on top of the head with her Bible. "I said, ain't that right, sucker? " She was ready to hit him again but my partner grabbed her wrist.

"That's enough. Don't hit him." I asked if she would sign a warrant for his arrest. If she did we would arrest the man.

"Damn straight, I'll sign papers to send this rogue to jail forever."

I looked down at the guy. "What about you? Do you have anything to say?"

He stared at the big woman and stuttered. "No, no sir, not now. I'll talk later."

We transported them to the Safety Building. The big lady signed the papers and I noticed in front of her name she wrote Bishop. I asked if she was a real bishop. She nodded, "For twenty-five years, honey. I'm a religious women but I don't take any bullshit from these thugs. They ruined my neighborhood. Anytime I can get a lick on one of them I'll rack his ass."

I must have looked confused because she asked. "What's the matter, honey?"

"Well, I talked to a lot of preachers and I never heard one cuss. How can you swear like that and be a bishop?"

"Cuss words were meant for the evil, no-goods that rob and kill people. You got to have nasty words for them. I'm sure the Lord understands and that's all that matters."

I laughed. I was getting to like this lady.

We took the robber to jail, then drove Bishop home. In the following days whenever she saw us she'd wave and we'd pull over. She'd fill us in on what was going on in the neighborhood. I told her this might not be a good idea being seen talking with us.

She shook her head. "Most of the people in this neighborhood are good. The scoundrels best be careful around me." She tapped her purse. "You see they know I also have something else in here besides my Bible."

We suspected what it was but we didn't ask. Best to leave well enough alone.

One day we were dispatched to Bishop's home. An elderly man and a young woman were standing on the sidewalk.

Bishop was on her front porch with clenched fists. We walked up and the couple shouted, "That big heifer insulted us."

Bishop came off the porch and started walking toward them. We stopped her. I asked,

"What's going on, Bishop?"

"They came to my house and wanted their fortune told."

"Wait a minute, Bishop. Are you a fortune teller?"

"Sure am. Been doing it for years. This old dude brought his young chick to my home. He said they were going to get married and wondered what the future held for him and his soon- to-be bride. Well, I know this girl. I told him. 'You don't want to know the future. You better learn about her past.' They both got mad and I threw them out of my home."

Bishop was a good honest person who wanted her neighborhood to be safe. We helped her every way we could. A lot of times when she told us something, I'd break out laughing because of the way she said it. I'd say, "Are you serious?"

She'd look straight in my eyes. "Honey, I'm as serious as a damn heart attack."

Bishop was the first person to call and congratulate me when I made detective. I asked her how she found out. She said, "Honey, you know I tell fortunes." This woman was full of surprises and humor. I liked her. She made me laugh.

One day I got a phone call from Bishop. She was excited. I asked her what was the matter.

"Tective, you got's to help me. "The rooster is back at my house,"

"What are you talking about? The rooster is at your house."

"I got's too many babies in this house, I don't need anymore. The rooster laid seed with my oldest daughter. Then he did the same with the middle girl. Now he is trying to lay seed with my youngest. I need some help or I'm going to put a stop to this no-good and I might end up in jail for the rest of my life."

I told her not to do anything. I got his name and I had a

long talk with him. He said he'd leave the family alone. I called Bishop and told her that he wouldn't come back to her chicken coop. She laughed and thanked me.

There wasn't a week that went by and Bishop would call and give me information. One night she called and said someone stole her barbeque grill. I asked if she had any suspects.

She said, "Honey, there's so many jitterbugs running through my backyard the ground gets hot. I don't know which low-life took it."

Another call. She kept yelling, "I bubbled him up. I bubbled him up." I couldn't get any more information, so I drove to her home. She saw me coming up the walk and ran out. "Tective Moosee, a no-good rogue done broke my window and was crawling in. I grabbed the kettle of hot potash I was boiling and I splashed it in his face. He jumped his sorry ass out the window, screaming."

Next I got a call from the dispatcher that a man entered the emergency room at Mercy Hospital with severe burns. I quickly drove to the hospital. I observed the man and he had blisters all over his face. He admitted to breaking into Bishop's home.

Years passed and Bishop's crime fighting slowed down. She gave me a real shock one day. I was in a crowded department store being measured for a suit. I was talking to the salesman when I heard this loud yell. "Tective Moosee."

I turned and there was Bishop about four aisles away waving. She shouted, "The doctor done took my titty."

I cringed and my shoulders went up to my ears. She started to yell again and I threw up my arms and shouted, "Hold it, Bishop, don't say anymore I'll be right there." I ran to her and she explained the whole operation in a lower voice.

Her condition must have worsened because I didn't hear from her anymore. One day I received a call from her daughter who told me Bishop passed away.

I went to the funeral home and looked at her. The worn Bible was on her chest with her hands over it. I could swear she smiled at me. I thought, the only thing missing was her pocketbook and the protection inside. I squinted when I heard her whisper. "Honey, where I'm at there's no rogues. I have no need for it."

I looked up with moist eyes and mumbled, "There'll never be another one like you Bishop. I'll miss you."

CHAPTER 47
CLOSE CALL

My friend Bill a college professor called and asked if I'd fill in for him for a couple days. He teaches police science and would like for me to instruct his students on interviewing and interrogation since I was a detective and dealt with it daily. He said, "Tell them how important it is to the investigation to get accurate information. Let them in on some of the secrets you have acquired over the years to get information."

I told him I would do my best. I was under the impression that the students in this class were young college kids who were interested in becoming police officers. My mind flashed back when I was in school. Some of the teachers were so boring it's a wonder anyone learned. I was determined not to be one of those dry teachers. My classes were going to be exciting and interesting.

I went to the school with my game plan. First, I went to the track coach and ask if I could borrow his starter pistol. He handed me the gun and I loaded it with blanks. I asked a male student if he would assist me in teaching my class. He asked what I wanted him to do and I explained my plan. "I want to startle the class just like a crime is being committed in front of them."

He looked confused. "So, what do you want me to do?"

"I will be teaching the class and I want you to come in with this starter pistol that shoots blanks. You yell, why did you give me that F on the last test? You ruined my point average. I'm going to kill you. You fire the gun at me and I'll duck under the desk. You then run from the room. After you leave I'll jump up and instruct five students to go out in the hall. I'll call them back in one at a time and ask them to explain what happened and to describe the shooter. I'll write each one's responses on the blackboard and then we'll compare their answers."

He nodded. "I get it. We want to scare them and in the excitement they won't be able to describe me. Just like when it really happens."

"Yeah, that's exactly what I want to do." We walked to the classroom and I handed him the starter gun. "Now you know what to do? I'll go over it again. Let me talk for about five minutes then you rush in and start shooting."

"I got it."

I walked into the classroom and felt pretty good for thinking up that skit. These students will never forget to separate the witnesses at the crime scene. I stood up in front of the room and introduced myself and explained I would be filling in for Professor Bill. I noticed some older guys in the class but didn't think much of it since I went back to college after getting discharged from the army.

I joked a little then started my speech on interviewing witnesses. I was stressing the point that in every group one person will have the most influence over the rest. It is best to quickly separate the witnesses or they might give a description of the suspect the same as the strong witness. I could tell they were interested in what I was saying because everyone was staring at me and no one was yawning.

Ten minutes into my speech the door flew open. In ran the student with the starter pistol in his hand. He aimed it at me and shouted. "You ruined my grade average by giving me that F on the last test." He fired the gun twice. I was getting ready to dive behind the desk when I saw five men jump up with revolvers in their hands aiming at the student. I realized now those older students were policemen who were taking the course. In unison, they shouted, "Freeze." The student threw the gun in the air and it struck the ceiling and fell to the floor.

He jumped behind me.

I shouted, "Whoa, whoa, hold your fire." The officers looked surprised as did the rest of the students. The kid behind me had his hands on my back. I could feel him shaking. I stood there with my hands out in front of me. I pointed at the officers. "Just take it easy and holster your weapons." This was an example, I will explain later. The off-duty police officers sat down.

The student who was behind me yelled, "Let me get my ass out of here." He rushed out the door.

I pointed at five students and told them to go out into the hall. I called them in one at a time and wrote on the board what they saw and their description of the suspect. The class was amazed how the five students' accounts of the incident varied so much.

After class was over the students gathered around my desk. One of them said. "Boy, you sure had me fooled. I thought that guy had a real gun. That was a great act. You really got my attention and drove that point home."

I nodded my head. "Thanks, I appreciate that. I hope you remember this class when you become an officer." I thought, I know, I will never forget it.

CHAPTER 48
YOU A MARINE?

Sergeant O'Hara was an ex-Marine on the police department for fifteen years. He was a quiet man until someone rubbed him wrong. A lot of the guys knew this and liked to tease him about being brained-washed in the Marines. Right away he would glare at them and yell, "The Marines brain-washed me into learning how to kick ass. Come on big mouth, let's go to the gym and put on the gloves." Many times he was taken up on the offer. He never backed down. The guys learned O'Hara loved the Marines and not to mess with him about it. The men respected him because he never expected them to do anything he wouldn't do. The man had guts and feared nothing.

The first time I met Sergeant O'Hara the prisoners in the jail were rioting and they took two guards hostage. O'Hara's eyes were squinting as he stared at the jail. The prisoners cursed and threatened him and the rest of the police officers outside.

Sergeant O'Hara turned to his men, "Okay, officers you heard them. It's time to go in and put this thing down. Form the V- Formation." We did and Sergeant O'Hara took the point position. This is the lead man and it's the most dangerous.

One of the officers shouted. "Sergeant, the captain and a hostage negotiator are on their way. Maybe we should wait for them."

"I ain't got time for a negotiator, and I don't have any faith in them. These losers only know one thing, force. So let's give it to them." He raised his hand over his head and yelled "Let's go." We entered the jail and the prisoners backed against the far wall.

Again, O'Hara put up his arm. We stopped. He pointed at the prisoners. "You drop all your weapons and get on your stomachs."

They didn't obey his orders. Instead they cursed, clenched their fists and threatened us to come and get them. O'Hara yelled, "It's head-cracking time. Get your clubs in the ready position." He turned to his men to make sure they were ready, then shouted, "Attack." We dove into the prisoners with clubs whaling. In a matter of a couple of minutes the prisoners were on their stomachs. One of them pointed at O'Hara and mumbled. "That man would kill."

Sergeant O'Hara ordered two prisoners to get up at a time. We then escorted them back to their cells. We found the two guard hostages and released them.

We were preparing to leave the area when the captain and the hostage negotiator showed up. The captain looked at Sergeant O'Hara, "Who gave you permission to storm this jail?"

O'Hara squinted. "I didn't need permission. There was a need and I took action."

The captain looked at the group of officers then back at O'Hara. "We'll solve this in the chief's office."

O'Hara shrugged his shoulders. He turned to the officers. "Great job, men."

Sergeant O'Hara's next escapade was when a man barricaded himself in his garage. He had an assortment of guns with him and yelling, "I'm going to kill myself and the first cop that tries to stop me." Officers took cover and surrounded the garage. The police negotiator was trying to persuade the guy to come out. The man kept making demands. First he wanted food. Then he wanted his wife. Then his preacher. Then he wanted his girlfriend. This stand-off went on and on with the man making more demands. The officers were ordered to stay put and let the negotiator handle the matter.

Sergeant O'Hara was on the other side of town in his scout car monitoring this. He mumbled to himself, "This has gone on long enough." He drove to the neighborhood where the incident was happening. He looked at the garage at the far end of the street He slammed the gas pedal down, tires squealed and smoked. "That's O'Hara someone yelled and he's headed for the garage." The speeding car went up the driveway became airborne and smashed into the large garage door exploding pieces of wood in every direction. A lot of cursing came from inside that garage, then Sergeant O'Hara came walking out with a handcuffed man. The man was shaking and pissed his pants.

O'Hara had to see the chief again. The chief reassigned him to a low crime district where noting exciting happened. It consisted of very rich people. He was ordered not to leave this district regardless what was happening in other parts of the city.

He was bored and hated this. Many times he thought of jumping a call but didn't because he knew the consequences. One day he was driving through an intersection and an old lady ran a red light and almost broadsided his scout car. She stopped inches away from his car. He got out and walked over to her. "Are you all right lady?"

"Never mind, just move that car. My husband is a very important man and he'll have your job if you don't."

O'Hara's blood pressure shot up. "Let me see your driver's license lady."

"I told you to get that car out of my way. Who do you think you are? I don't have time for your foolishness."

"Listen, Bitch, show me your drivers license or I'll pull your sorry ass out of that car and throw you in jail."

"Oh, oh." Her hands shook and fumbled in her purse. She handed him the license.

O'Hara looked at it then handed it back. He felt sorry for her and gave her a break.

The following day he was back in the chief's office. The chief shook his head. "You're a good officer, O'Hara, but you got to understand you're not in the Marines anymore. Your new assignment is booking officer in the jail. Hold your temper. Understand?"

O'Hara shook his head, gritted his teeth and said, "Yes, Sir."

O'Hara worked behind the booking counter. Prisoners were brought in and he had to question them before placing them in cells. He hated talking to drunks because they had bad breath. They liked to get close to his face when they talked. O'Hara would turn his head and shout, " Back off, get out of my face." He got tired of yelling at them so he brought in a four-foot stick and he'd shoved it in their chest when they talked to him.

One night O'Hara almost blew his top. An arrested man dressed in a white formal, long blond wig, falsies and high heeled-shoes was brought in. The guy was drunk, giddy and talked in a very feminine manner. The arresting officers directed him to the booking counter in front of O'Hara. The guy looked at O'Hara, "Oh my, look at the big strong sergeant."

O'Hara pointed at the arresting officers. "Get this broad the hell out of here. "

The officer smiled. "It isn't a woman. It's a man."

O'Hara glared at the prisoner trying to figure out what to say.. Someone yelled. "He's a Marine on furlough from Paris Island."

O'Hara jumped over the counter and was now standing directly in front of the guy in the formal. "Come to attention, you." The guy straightened up but wobbled because of the high heels. O'Hara shouted, "Are you a Marine?"

The guy raised a limp hand. "Oh, no, no, my, gosh no."

O'Hara kept staring at him then said. "Your lucky your not."

CHAPTER 49
DANGEROUS ANIMAL

I got off duty and walked out of the Safety Building. Someone yelled my name and I stopped and turned. Running up was Jim Ray. We were both rookies and starting to ride with older officers. When he got close he was shaking his head. "Bob, you worked with Dave Maher, didn't you? I heard about when he wore that long blond wig and sent people to Bruno's exterminators with cockroaches and Bruno almost blew a gasket."

"Yeah, that Maher is quite a guy. It's a real experience working with him. He has a funny way of answering calls."

"Tell me about it. I worked with him a couple days ago. Get this. After roll call I went to the car and was checking out the equipment. I noticed this large yellow wood box with red writing on the side, sitting on the back seat. The words were in a foreign language. On top of the box, bold letters in English said, **DANGEROUS ANIMAL - STAY CLEAR.**

"Man, I stood my distance from that damn thing but my curiosity got the best of me. I leaned in the car and looked inside that box and there was this furry thing. I backed away and waited for Maher. When he came, I pointed at the box. He stared at me for the longest time, then slowly shook his head. Cautiously, he reached inside the car and slid the box out.

"He said, 'We got to be careful because there is a mongoose inside and it's mean as hell. We have to transport it to the zoo.' All the time he was telling me about this animal, he kept his face away from the cage like he was scared of it. 'You, got to be careful because this thing will rip your face off.' He motioned for me to get closer. I slowly bent over; when I looked inside, he pulled a lever which released a spring that made the top of the cage fly open with a loud bang. A large piece of fur hooked to the top of the cage sprung out and clung to my face. Bob, I was so scared I almost shot the damn thing. That fool Maher stood there and laughed. I was ready to punch him, but didn't.

"But that wasn't the end of it. The screwball took it on calls with us. Once we answered a large street disturbance and he walked into the crowd carrying the box. The people became quiet, their eyes were fixed on the box. Maher kept talking to the inside of that box as if trying to calm down whatever was inside. He looked at the people and said. 'I'm sorry I have this cage with me. We were on our way to the zoo to take this ferocious animal back. It's so mean and dangerous we can't leave the box out of our sight for fear it will escape again. It's maimed a few people already. The last person it attacked, it tore the guy's nose and ears off. Please, let's get this disturbance settled so we can return this terrible thing to the zoo.'

"No one said a word why they called us. They just stared at the box and asked questions about the animal. Maher kept talking, making the animal seem more fierce. One guy got brave and cautiously walked up to the box to get a look. Maher kept warning him not to get too close, but the guy kept coming. He leaned over to see, when Maher pulled the lever. Man, that fur flew out of that box and landed on the guy's face. His false teeth flew out of his mouth. He screamed, 'Help, it got me. Get it off.' He rolled all over the ground.

"Everyone laughed. Maher stood there with a big smile. A woman pointed at Maher and said, 'That's that crazy policeman I told you about. Man, you don't know what that cat is going to do.' Maher set the spring to the cage again. He looked at the people and asked, if anyone else wanted a close look at the mongoose. There were no takers. They backed away and laughed. The disturbance was over. They forgot what they were fighting about. We walked back to our car and the crowd dispersed.

"Next we had to serve some warrants. We got a tip from one of Maher's snitches that the guy we were looking for was in a pool hall. We didn't know what he looked like. Maher drove to a phone booth about a half block away from the pool hall. He got on the phone and said, 'I want to speak to Leon Smith; it's very important.'

" Whoever answered got Leon. Maher tells the guy, 'Man, you best get out of there. The cops are on the way to arrest you.'

"Maher got back in the car and pointed at a guy running out of the pool hall. He laughed and said, 'That's the guy. You get out of the car and I'll go around the block. When he sees the car, he'll turn and run. That's when you grab him.'

" I got out and hid behind a tree. Maher drove around the block and when he came around the corner he blew the siren. The guy jumped in the air then ran right into my arms.

"Bob, I don't understand anything this Maher does. Sometimes I think he's crazy but other times I think he's a genius. It's a real experience working with him. You don't know what he's going to do next.

"I asked Maher why he answers calls this way. He said, 'One of these crazy drunken nuts out here can snuff your lights out in a second. You got to out think them and keep them off balance. You mess with their minds and they get confused. That's what you want to do. Keep them confused. It's better than being shot or fighting.'

"I then asked if the command ever wrote him up for acting this way. He said, 'If you notice this district is the meanest. No command stays in this area long. They don't want to get involved with these crazies. But if they did give me a problem, I'd mess with their minds, too. They also think I'm a bubble-off so they don't want anything to do with a nut.'

"Bob, I just looked at him and shrugged my shoulders. If you worked with that guy for any length of time you'd end up talking to yourself."

"I know what you mean, Jim. You mentioned serving

warrants. I'll tell you what he did, when I was working with him. We had a warrant for a James Johnson. We went to the address and a guy answered the door. Maher looked at him and asks, 'Are you Carl Cox?' I almost screwed up and was going to correct Maher and tell him we wanted a James Johnson.

"The guy said, 'I'm not Carl Cox.'

"Maher says, 'I know you're Carl Cox.' The guy quickly pulls out his wallet and shows Maher his driver's license that said he was James Johnson.

Maher slapped the cuffs on him and says, 'You'll do.'

He then shows the guy the warrant and the guy yells. 'Man, this is some shit'."

I laughed. "Jim, Maher is unorthodox but he gets the job done. He's worked Unit 10, the roughest district, for thirteen years and survived. Most guys would be dead or in the cracker factory jabbering to themselves after working that area for so long."

"Yeah, I can understand that, Bob. But I'm not looking forward to working with him again."

CHAPTER 50
I DON'T WANT ANY TROUBLE

John Britz was a teenager. He was short, about five-foot-four and weighed about a hundred-thirty pounds. He had black hair that hung over his forehead in bangs. He wore dark horned-rimmed glasses and when he got nervous he giggled. He didn't participate in sports like the other guys in the neighborhood. It was thought he didn't have enough energy because his mother skimmed on his meals. John liked to hang around with the wilder boys. He knew they would make him laugh with the crazy stunts they pulled. He stayed around until they'd do something that might get him in trouble. John did everything possible to stay out of trouble. But trouble stuck to him.

It seemed this trouble started when John was eight years old. His older brothers who were ten and twelve took a razor and shaved all the hair from his head and then shaved off his eyebrows. Later that day John was standing on a corner watching the cars go by. A woman driving and making a right hand turn saw John's bald head and how funny he looked without any eyebrows. She kept staring at him and crashed into a telephone pole. She got out of the car and shouted, "You bald headed looking little freak you caused me to wreck my car." John got nervous and giggled. The woman screamed, "I ought to slap you for laughing." John couldn't understand why she acted that way. He didn't do anything wrong.

When he became a teenager he and four other boys were walking through River Side Park. Charlie Wagner had just finished drinking a bottle of Coke. Charlie raised the thick glass bottle and pointed down hill to a large clump of high weeds. "Hey you guys, do you think I can throw this bottle all the way into those weeds?" Everyone watched as he swung his arm a couple of times to warm it up. He then shouted, "Here it goes."

The bottle flew a high arc then came down in the middle of the weed patch. It didn't make a swishing noise like it should have as it went though the weeds, instead it made a loud clunk followed by a scream "Ow! Son-of-a-bitch." A man jumped up holding his head. A woman periscoped her head out of the high weeds. The guy stumbled from the weeds pulling up his pants, rubbing his head and shouting, "I'll kill you bastards." He started charging up the hill with fists clenched.

One of the boys yelled. "Let's get out of here. That guy is mad."

Everyone ran except John Britz.

The other boys looked back, "Come on John that guy will kick your ass."

John shook his head. "I'm not running because I didn't do anything."

The boys kept shouting for him to run. John just stood there. The man was getting closer rubbing his head, charging and snorting like a bull. They yelled again for John to run. He didn't, but they did.

The next day the boys were sitting on Charlie's front porch. John Britz came walking up. He was holding one half of his glasses over an eye. His other eye was black. The boys said in unison. "We told you to run. What happened?"

"Man, that guy was crazy. I tried to explain but I got nervous and giggled. He got madder and started punching. I fought him the best I could. My glasses broke and I could hardly see him. Lucky the cops came and broke us up. They told us to go our separate ways. I left because I didn't want any trouble."

Everyone was laughing and shaking their heads. A horn blew and a large white truckwith "TONY'S HOT POPCORN," written on the side parked in front of the house. The door opened and Ivan Briscoff, better known as Ivan the Terrible, came out. He walked up to the guys. "You want to go swimming at the quarry? I got a job from Tony and I don't start until tonight."

The group on the porch jumped up and raced home for their swim trunks. Once back and inside the truck with their trunks on Ivan started to pull away. Charley shouted. "Hold it, Ivan, I want to go back in my house." When he came out, he was carrying a picnic ham. "I took it out of the oven, my mother was cooking it for supper. It will taste good after we get done swimming." On the way to the quarry Ivan told them to eat all the popcorn they wanted. At the quarry everyone except John Britz raced to the water and dove in.

After a couple of hours they got out of the water and crowded around the ham. Charlie grabbed it and all that was left was a large bone. He looked at John and noticed his swim-trunks weren't wet. Charlie pointed at him. "You ate the whole ham."

John shook his head and all the time picking his teeth. "Not me."

On the way home they had to stop on the Ash Street Bridge because the span was open to let a large freighter through. It was quiet since all the boys were stuffing popcorn in their mouths. All at once Ivan sat straight up in the driver's seat. "Man we're in trouble."

Someone asked. "What do you mean?"

"Well, I really didn't get a job from Tony. I stole his truck. Look on the other side of the bridge. There's a police car. I bet the cops are waiting for the bridge to close and then they're going to arrest us."

The truck door flew open and John Britz jumped out and climbed the railing to the bridge. The bridge-tender saw him and shouted over the microphone. "Get off that railing! Don't jump!" It was too late. John was already in the air falling down to the water.

The police officers must have seen him jump. The red

flasher lights to their car went on and did an U-turn and drove to the dirt road under the bridge and waited for John to swim to shore.

Everyone in the truck gave a sigh of relief. Ivan drove the popcorn truck off the bridge and parked it. He yelled, "Lets get the hell out of here." The boys ran in different directions.

The officers asked John why he jumped off the bridge. He told them he did it on a dare. They drove him home and told his mother. He got worse punishment from her then if he had gone to court.

John was now really paranoid about getting in trouble. He stayed to himself until one day the boys asked if he wanted to go to the neighborhood theater with them. He thought, there couldn't be much of a chance getting in trouble watching a movie, so he went.

The boys were all sitting in the same row. Everyone was enjoying the show. Bill Taylor whispered in Charley's ear. "Watch me scare John. He took a large firecracker out of his pocket. He then elbowed John who was sitting on the other side of him and said, "I'm going to light this in here. Would you hold the match?"

John's head was shaking. "Are you crazy? Man, let me the hell out of here." He got up and ran to a seat six rows up. Every once in awhile he would look back.

Bill Taylor and Charley laughed every time he did it. Bill then struck a match and was faking like he was going to light the big firecracker. Charley kept telling him to put it away.

The movie got exciting and Bill looked up and didn't realize the flame of the match lit the wick.

He looked down and saw the wick spitting sparks. He tried to pinch it out. The wick was too thick and he couldn't stop it. It was ready to go off so he threw it in the air and it exploded right above John Britz's head. There was a brilliant flash and a loud bang. The house lights went on and the theater filled with smoke. People ran down the aisles and outside.

The manager was on the stage shouting, trying to calm everyone. A lady pointed at John. "That guy that looks like an owl did it. He threw it."

John's nervous giggle started. He shook his head and yelled, "Bullshit." And ran.

******

Eight years later John Britz became an usher in a theater. This day the movie was, "The Greatest Story Ever Told." They were going to crucify the Lord. John stopped in the aisle and stared at the show. He became nervous and began to giggle. A woman jumped up from her seat and smacked him with her purse and shouted, "You sick jerk." A man took a punch at him. Other people got up and started closing in on John. He ran out the front door.

The police were called. John calmed down and thought he could explain his nervous condition to the police and the matter would be solved.

The squad car pulled up and the officers got out. John ran to them. One officer squinted and looked at John funny. He pointed and said. "Hey! I remember you, you're the one who wacked that guy with a coke bottle who was diddling that broad in the bushes."

The woman who hit John with her purse yelled, "I knew he was a pervert."

John shook his head, giggled and ripped off the usher uniform. He threw it on the ground and yelled, "Screw this, I quit." John joined the Marines. It would be interesting to know how He got along with his drill instructor at boot camp.

CHAPTER 51
IT AIN'T WHAT IT LOOKS LIKE

It was three-thirty in the morning and we had run fifteen calls and most of them were mean and physical. Things slowed down and it felt good. The drunks, must all be home sleeping it off. Frank my partner looked over. "What you say we get a couple of coffees and go to a quiet spot to catch our breaths?" I nodded and he drove to an all night restaurant. We knew the owner and I went in the back door directly into the kitchen.

John, the cook, smiled and said, "Man, I've been listening to the police radio and you guys were running your asses off. This town sounded like it was going crazy. What can I do for you, Bob?"

"Just a couple of coffees to go." He filled two Styrofoam cups with coffee and threw a couple of hot rolls in a bag. I took out my wallet to pay.

"Put your money away. Having you guys coming in here during the nights is great. Those scum-bags who see your car think twice before they try to hold up the place." I thanked him and left.

Frank drove to a closed gas station and parked in a dark spot. I opened the bag and handed Frank his coffee. He didn't take the cup. Instead he shouted "Damn, I knew this quiet was too good to be true." He pointed to a guy running down the sidewalk with a television on his shoulder. I jumped from the car and chased the guy.

I shouted for him to stop. He turned and saw my uniform, dropped the television and ran faster. With red lights flashing,

Frank blocked him. The guy stopped and I ordered him on the ground. He looked up at me. "Officer Bob, man, give me some slack. The judge will send my ass to jail forever. I'll tell you the whole thing if you give me a break."

I shook my head. "Willie, you know what the judge said the last time. I'm sure he'll send you away. Let's hear what you got to say. We don't want any bullshit. You understand?"

"No man, this is straight. I was walking down the street and I saw this house with the TV on. All at once it went off and the house got dark. I figured the guy went to bed and I would break in and take his TV. I broke a window on the side of the house and reached in and took the TV. Man, I didn't go in. I just reached in the window and pulled it out."

"What house did you take it from?"

"It's a couple of blocks back that way."

"If we drive you there will you point out the house?"

"Sure will."

Willie got in the back seat and directed us. He pointed to a house and said, "That's the one." I got out of the car and went to the home. I shone my flashlight on my hat and pounded on the door. The door slowly opened and a middle-aged guy in his undershorts appeared.

"Yeah, what's the problem?"

"A guy broke into your home a while ago and took your TV. We got your TV and the guy in the car."

"I don't know what you mean. No one broke into my home." He slowly turned and looked in his front room. He got a surprised expression. He stuttered, "Man, I don't own a TV."

I was confused. "Hey, did you hear me, we got your TV and the guy who took it in the car."

"Hey, like I said, I don't own a TV."

I walked back to the car and pointed at Willie. "Why you giving us the run around? The guy said there was no break in and he don't own a TV."

"The man's a liar." He pointed at the house. "I took the TV out of that house."

"Okay, get out of the car and show me the broken window." Willie got out, my partner and I held him by his belt. He led us to a broken window on the side of the house. Most of the shattered glass was on the inside which told us the window was broken from the outside.

The guy who answered the door was now standing behind us. I shone my flashlight on the broken window. "How do you explain that?"

"My old lady got pissed and threw a lamp at me and it missed and broke the window." He gave Willie a mean look and said, "Why you putting the mouth on me?" Willie smiled and shrugged his shoulders.

Frank and I were confused. I asked the guy where his wife was when she threw the lamp. He said, "She was standing in the middle of the front room." I went to the car and got the serial numbers off the TV set and checked with the Record Bureau. The report came back the TV was stolen. It was taken in a burglary three weeks ago. I walked back and pointed at the guy from the house. "You're not claiming that TV because it's hot. We're going to have an investigation to see if the owner wants to press charges. And since you say your wife broke the window we'll have to let Willie here go free." I nodded at Willie. He didn't hesitate. He took off running.

We placed the TV in the police property room with a request for a follow up investigation.

CHAPTER 52
NEVER GIVE UP

I've played on many football teams and met a lot of players. None played as hard and so fiercely as Mike Tackas. He stood six foot three and weighed two hundred and forty pounds. My position was quarterback, also known as the field general. In other words, the leader of the team while on the field. Mike played tackle, one of the roughest positions. His job was to move opposing players so our men carrying the ball could get through the line. He also protected the quarterback when he was passing the ball. Mike did it well.

In all the games we played Mike never questioned any decision I made. He kept quiet in the huddle. Whatever I said, he'd nod and carry out his assignment. The man was living terror for opposing teams. He never gave up, no matter what the odds or the score was.

After the games were over Mike Tackas turned into a different person. He was soft spoken and well mannered, until...and I say "Until" he went into a bar and drank whiskey. He picked up the nickname, Bar Sweeper. When people saw him order whiskey they quickly exited. Those that remained were at their own peril.

In St. Louis we were invited to a party by the opposing team. We played a hard game against them and won by one point. After the game, both teams showed good sportsmanship by shaking hands. The conversation was friendly and we congratulated each other on what a tough game they played.

We took showers and went to the party. I saw Mike start drinking Depth Charges. He would take double shots of whiskey and drop the small shot glass into a large mug of beer. He than shook the mug tipping the whiskey into the beer and bringing the mug to his mouth and chugging it. He did a couple of these Depth Charges and I went to the far end of the hall.

An hour passed and I heard a loud yell from the bar area. I recognized Mike's voice.

"We kicked your ass on the field and we can do it again. Right here, now."

I thought, *Here we go again.* Lucky a few of our larger players were standing close by and they quickly got him out of there and kept him on our bus until the rest of us could board it and go home.

I was getting older, I retired from football and became a police officer and didn't see Mike Tackas for at least three years. I was working in uniform with a partner on a scout car. We along with another crew were dispatched to a large bar fight. We pulled up to the bar and a woman came running up. She shouted, "Mike Tackas is tearing up my bar." She pointed at two big guys who were rubbing their wounds. "He punched both of them and threw them out on the sidewalk. He's wild and is destroying my place."

The other crew pulled up. I told my partner and the other officers that I knew the guy inside and I can handle him. The owner of the bar looked at me. "Honey. You don't understand. That guy in there is big and tough. You better take your buddies with you."

The other officers were nodding. I put up my hands. "Listen, let me go in there. You watch through the windows and if I need help, rush in. Just give me a chance with him."

I walked in and Mike was behind the bar. He had pulled the sink off the wall in the men's restroom and was bashing the bottles on the back bar with it. I sat on a stool and said, "Hey, I want a beer."

He didn't turn around. He kept smashing the sink into the bottles. He shouted, "Screw you."

I yelled, "Hey! I want a beer."

He slowly turned and stared at me for a long time. "Bobby, what you doing in that uniform?"

"I became a cop after football. How you been, Mike?"

He slowly bent down and put the sink on the floor, all the while watching me. "Hey, Mike, I asked for a beer."

"Bobby, you can't drink in that uniform. You'll get in trouble. You know better than that." He slowly came around the bar and sat on the stool next to me. "It's great seeing you, Bobby. Man. We had some great times. You remember when we played that Detroit team and beat them? They were supposed to whip us. They got mad and we had that big fight on the field afterwards, and they had to call the law to stop it. Man, that was a riot."

"Yeah I remember. Those were the good days. Tell me Mike, why you tearing up this place?"

"Oh, I don't know. I was restless and started drinking whiskey and You know what that does to me. I know the broad that owns this bar. I'll pay for the damage and everything will be all right."

"I don't know. She looked really mad. If I bring her in here, will you talk with her and not get crazy? Maybe we can get this settled."

"Sure Bobby, I'm all right."

I went outside. The owner came up to me. "I don't believe you calmed him down. He was really wild tonight. I like the guy when he's sober. He'll give you anything he's got. But when he gets whiskey in him all hell breaks loose." I asked if she wanted to prosecute him. She said, "All I want now, is for him to leave. I don't want to talk to him until I know for sure all that firewater is out of him."

I looked for the two guys Mike had punched, they had left. I went back into the bar.

He was still sitting on the stool. I walked up to him. "Mike the deal is this. We're going to take you home and tomorrow you come back here and settle up with the owner for the damages."

"That sounds fair to me."

I led the way to the scout car and Mike had his hand on my shoulder laughing and talking about the good old times.

Everything must of turned out all right because we didn't hear anymore about it. Two months later, we were called to the Toledo Mental Hospital. It was three in the morning. Mike was standing inside a room that had a large broken window. He had pulled a stop sign out of the ground, smashed the window and crawled inside. He kept shouting, "I want to commit myself." He looked at me, "Bobby, the booze got the best of me and I got to beat it."

I shook his hand. "I'm glad Mike. But for God's sake the next time wait until the place is open."

Many years passed and I didn't see Mike again. I heard he quit drinking completely. I retired from the police department and moved to Florida. One day I got a phone call from Toledo, Ohio. The guy said he was from Alcoholic Anonymous. Right away I said, "Wait a minute. I don't have a problem"

"I understand. Would you do our organization a favor? We know you're a friend of Mike Tackas." I was waiting for him to say Mike tore up the place. Instead he said. "Mike is dying of cancer and is in bad shape. We heard Mike tell stories and you were in every one of them. He thinks a lot of you. Would you please give him a call? I'm sure, if he hears your voice it would perk him up."

"Sure, I'll call him. Give me his number." I dialed the number and Mike's wife answered. She said, "Mike is bedridden, thin and very weak. He is sleeping and I don't want to wake him up." I told her who I was.

"Oh, Bobby. I saw so many games the Tornadoes played; you guys had a great team. Wait, I'll bring the phone to Mike. He'll want to talk with you."

A very weak voice like a low rasping whisper said, "Hello, who is this?"

I don't know why, but I got the urge to mess with him. I said in a mean voice. "Never mind who I am. Are you the Mike Tackas who played tackle for the Toledo Tornadoes?"

"Yeah, I played five years for the Tornadoes."

"Well, I've been looking for you for twenty years. I played for the Pittsburgh Iron Dukes and when we were playing, you hit me with a forearm that broke my nose and knocked out my front teeth. Now I found you, I'm going to kick your ass."

Mike's response was immediate. The weak voice now was strong. He shouted. "Listen, son-of-a-bitch. I live at 1210 Martin St. I'll pay for your taxi. I'll be waiting in my front yard." *(I can't tell the rest of the words he shouted.)*

It took me ten minutes to calm him down and convince him it was me. He then laughed and said. "I'll pay **your** taxi. Come over here and I'll kick your ass for tricking me."

We had a long talk and I felt good that I could cheer up an old friend and teammate. Mike died two weeks later.

CHAPTER 53
OLD MAN AND THE FIRE

Frank and I were on normal patrol. He was driving and looked over at me. "Bob, I don't think we're going to get much business tonight. It's just too damn cold. I bet if you got out of the car and took a leak you'd have to walk backwards."

I laughed, "You're right there. It's nice to have a day when we can sit back and take it easy." I no sooner spoke when a woman came running down the sidewalk screaming and flailing her arms. We both rushed out of the car. She grabbed the front of my shirt. I yelled, "Calm down lady. What's the matter?"

She pointed to a house. "That house is on fire. There's an old, blind man inside."

"What room is he in?"

"He stays in the front room. When you enter the front door you'll see him."

As we ran to the house we heard the fire trucks sirens wailing. Orange and red light was flickering in the front window of the home. We looked inside and saw an old man, in long-johns smoking a pipe in an overstuffed chair. The rug the chair sat on was burning. Flames were dancing all around him.

We tried the door but it was locked. We pounded on it and yelled. No one answered. We both drove our shoulders into the door and it flew open. We ran in and now were standing in front of the old man. He continued smoking his pipe nonchalantly. We yelled at him but he didn't respond. Evidently he was hard of hearing too. All at once he shrugged his shoulders and yelled. "Close the damn door I feel a draft. I'm cold."

We grabbed the chair with the old guy in it and managed to wrestle it through the door.

He yelled all the time. We lowered it in the front yard. He shivered, swore and clinched his fists.

"You damn fools, what the hell is the matter with you? What's going on? You only sit outside in the summer. Put me back in my house. I'm freezing." I ran to the car and got our emergency blanket and covered him.

Frank laughed. "Bob did you notice all the time he was yelling and cussing, he never took the pipe out of his mouth. I bet a spark from his pipe started that fire."

The fire trucks pulled up and in no time the fire was out. A car screeched to a stop and a woman ran up to us. "Please, tell me what happened." She pointed to the old man in the chair. "That's my father. Is he all right?"

We assured her he was okay. She bent over and stuck her finger in his chest. From the expression on his face he knew who it was. She yelled in his ear. "I told you a million times not to smoke that damn pipe when I'm not home."

The old man had a sheepish look. He squinted and nodded his head. "Yeah, yeah."

The smoke cleared from the house and we carried him back in. His daughter dropped to her knees and looked everywhere within arms distance from the over stuffed chair. She found two more pipes, tobacco and matches. She held them in the palms of her hand. "Officers, please tell me how a man in his condition can hide these things? He is impossible." She thanked us and we left.

Back in the car Frank had a serious look. "Bob did you ever think that some day that might be us sitting in that chair smoking a pipe."

I laughed. "Not me I don't smoke."

CHAPTER 54
THAT'S LIFE

My partner and I were sitting in the car making out reports. The Dispatcher came over the radio. "Unit Eleven, we received a call that a car drove off the Middle Grounds Pier into the river. Check it out. Step it up"

We okayed the call, slapped our report pads closed and flipped on the red lights and siren. In a matter of minutes we screeched to a stop at the dock. The only one there was an old black man fishing. We ran up to him and I shouted. "Sir, did you call the police?"

He didn't take his eyes off his poles. "Nope."

I looked at Frank and he shrugged his shoulders and showed his palms. "Nothing must have happened here, Bob. Probably a phony call."

We started to walk back to our car and for some reason I turned and yelled at the old guy. "Did you see a car drive off into the water?"

The guy kept his eyes on his poles and said, "Yeah."

We ran back to him. I yelled again. "Where did it go in?"

He looked up then pointed at the river about ten feet from where he was fishing. "Right there." His eyes went back to his poles. "I ain't had a bite since the fool did it."

Frank yelled, "Fool? Was there a man in the car when it went in? Tell us about it."

The old guy slowly pulled a billfold from his chest pocket of his bib overalls and handed it to me. "Here the dude gave it to me." He looked back at his poles and didn't say anymore.

"Hey! Tell us what happened after he gave you the wallet.

What did the guy say to you? Did he look like he was drunk?"

The old guy made a face like we were bothering him. He hesitated then said, "Well, he got back in his car and backed it up as far as he could." The old fisherman pointed to some buildings about a hundred yards away. "The car made a loud noise and the tires started squealing and smoking. The next thing I saw was the car flying in the air and it made a big splash. I haven't had a bite since."

Frank asked if the guy who was driving came to the surface after the car went in the water.

"Man, I didn't look. I was watching my poles. I don't have time for that nonsense."

We called the rescue squad and the divers went in and pulled the driver from the car. He was dead. We opened the billfold and inside was the guy's personal papers, money and a suicide note. Frank and I read it. *"I've had enough, this life is not fair."*

Frank shook his head. "I guess he got his wish."

A huge tow truck lifted the car from the river. Water and dirt cascaded from it. The old guy picked up his fishing gear and put it in a broken down shopping cart. He had a disgusted look. Slowly he walked away pushing the cart. He mumbled. "It ain't going to be good fishing here for a long time."

The driver of the car was loaded into a transport vehicle to be taken to the city morgue. Our eyes went back and forth from the old man pushing the shopping cart to the black vehicle with dark windows driving away. Frank shook his head and said. "That's life, get use to it."

CHAPTER 55
CONFESSION

Every police department has a few. From the first day on the department they become obsessed in being promoted. They hang around the civil service office where the promotional tests are being made up, in hopes of getting a morsel of information that will give them an edge over the other guys on the next test. You see them come to work with briefcases filled with books so they can study while they're working. Instead of patrolling their districts looking for crime, they find a secluded spot, park the car and read promotional test books. The only time they get involved with crime is when the dispatcher sends them on a call.

I had an interesting situation involving one of these officers. He was a captain bucking for deputy chief. He'd enter his office when he started work and never came out until it was time to go home. His whole day was spent behind closed doors studying for the next test.

One day a man walked into the detective bureau from the street. He said he was a serial killer and wanted to confess. Lieutenant Sood tapped me on the shoulder while I was typing out reports.

"Bob, I think we got something big. There's a guy who says he killed a lot of people and wants to get it off his chest. How about sitting down with him and find out what's going on?"

I agreed and took the man into the interrogation room. He was about six feet tall and must have weighed around two hundred pounds. He was clean shaven and soft spoken. I asked him what he wanted to talk about. He shook his head a couple of times then looked down at the desk.

"I did some terrible things and it's bothering me. I want to tell you the whole story. I don't care what the consequences are."

I nodded. "Okay, let's hear what you got to say. If I can help you, I will."

"It started a month ago in Los Angeles. I shot and killed a cop. I robbed a gas station and an officer got behind my car and turned on his red lights and siren. I pulled over and knew he was going to arrest me. When he came up to my window, I shot him in the face. I then drove to a crowded neighborhood and ditched my car on a side street. I hot-wired a 1960 Blue Chevrolet and drove around until I found another1960 Chevrolet. I exchanged the license plates from the cars. I figured the guy who owned the car would never realize he was driving around with stolen plates. The police would be looking for the license plates on his car. There was only one problem. The car I was driving was blue and the license plates came off a black car.

I went to a hardware store and bought eight spray cans of black paint. I drove into the desert and painted the car black. Running short on money outside of Las Vegas I robbed a motel. The guy studied my face and I knew he was going to call the cops to identify me. I shot him, and I'm sure I killed him, because I hit him in the chest by his heart."

"How much money did you get?"

"Only thirty-five dollars. I drove about a hundred miles and found a pay phone. I called a cab. Before the cab got there, I lifted the hood of the car and made it appear it had broken down. The cab pulled up and I got in. I told him I wanted all his money. He didn't cooperate so I shot him in the back of his neck. I took his wallet and there was forty dollars inside. I kept his personal papers in case I needed fake identification.

I drove into Vegas and parked my car on a side street. I went into the casinos and watched until I saw a guy win a lot of money. I waited until he left and I followed him on foot. When he got to a secluded area, I ran up behind him and hit him on the head with the butt of my gun. The guy went down and I took his winnings. He started coming to, so I shot him twice in the head. I ran back to my car and drove all the way to Lincoln, Nebraska. Again I was running short on money. I noticed a bank early one morning. A lone man unlocked the door and went inside. I figured he was the manager. A half hour later the tellers started showing up and each time the manager unlocked the door for them.

The next morning I hid in some high bushes near the door of the bank. The manager showed up and put the key in the door. I rushed out of the bushes and put my gun in his back and shoved him inside. I ordered him to lock the door again and he did. I warned him if he pushed a secret alarm and the police showed up, I would kill him.

We went into the vault and I filled a bag with hundred dollar bills. I tied up the guy and put him in the vault so he wouldn't see me drive away. As I was leaving, I figured the manager could identify me so I went back and shot him. I drove all day. It was getting dark. I called on a pay phone and had a guy deliver food from a restaurant. I met him on the street so he wouldn't see my car. I then went to a camping park. I didn't want to talk to anyone but these people kept bugging me to come to their campfire. I went to the fire and they looked at me funny. I thought they recognized me and might call the cops. I excused myself and went back to my car and got my three-fifty-seven revolver. On the way back to the campfire I released the safety. I snuck up behind them and shot all four in the back of the head."

I put up my hands. "Could you wait a minute and excuse me? I just remembered something I forgot to do before we started talking."

He stood up. "Wait a minute there's a lot more."

"I know, but this is important and it will only take a little time."

He was reluctant to let me leave but he sat down and said,

"Well, okay."

I knew something was wrong with his story when he said he released the safety on the revolver. It hit me like an electrical shock. Revolvers don't have safeties. I called the Los Angeles Police Department and talked to a detective in homicide. I asked him if an officer in his department had been shot and killed in the last six months. He said no. I then explained to him about the subject who was confessing to a string of murders across the United States.

He sort of laughed. "Tell me, does this guy have receding red hair and does he lisp when he talks?"

"Yeah, that sounds like him."

"Go check the back of his neck and see if there's a small tattoo of a devil holding a pitchfork?"

I told him to hang on and I went back to the interrogation room. The guy looked up at me and started confessing some more. I pulled the collar of his shirt down and there was the tattoo of the devil. I went back to the phone. "Yeah, this guy has a devil on the back on his neck."

The officer laughed. "You got Milford Renard. He's very convincing and can lie like hell. Don't believe a thing he says. He must have come to our department and confessed twenty times to crimes. Whenever the newspapers gives a lot of print to a crime old Milford shows up the next day to confess to it. It's very time consuming to check out everything he says because one time he might do it. Hey! Will you do me a favor?"

"Sure, what do you want?"

"Will you please keep that crackpot in Toledo?"

As I walked back to the interrogation room, mumbling what I was going call this guy, Lieutenant Sood grabbed my arm. "How's it going, Bob?"

I started to tell him when the Captain came out of his office. "Bob. The news papers and the TV stations are driving me crazy calling about a serial killer confessing to a lot of murders. Is that true?"

"Yes sir."

"Well, I know you'll be working on this case late into the night. I need you to take emergency cases that might come in. I'll take over this one. Just go back to your desk and work on whatever you were doing before this came in."

I looked at Lieutenant Sood and then back at the Captain. "Yes Sir. Do you want me to make out a supplemental report of what I did so far?"

"No, that won't be necessary. I'll handle it from the start to the finish. We don't want too many names on the report. It will be confusing when the case goes to court."

I was going to tell him about the phone call to Los Angeles. But he said he wanted to take it from start to finish. He quickly went into the interrogation room. I stood there with the Lieutenant who said. "Bob, I'm sorry about this. He found out this investigation was going to get a lot of publicity. That's the only reason he put his books down and came out of the office. He'll do anything to get attention for a promotion."

I smiled, and told him about the phone call to Los Angeles.

"Aw, ain't that great. You made my day."

When I left work five hours later, the captain was still in the interrogation room talking to Milford. I called the news media and told them the serial killer investigation was so serious a captain is now handling the case. Of course, I didn't give my name.

CHAPTER 56
SWANS

Everything had changed since Ted's father, a policeman, was killed answering a robbery in progress call. He missed his father. Anytime he had a problem he could go to him and get a straight answer. His father taught him the importance of being respectful of other people and never be a bully. These morals were rooted in him since he was a young child.

The police pension helped but his mother knew it wouldn't cover all the expenses. She received a job offer from another city and they had to move. Ted felt bad about going for many reasons but the worse was he had to leave the football team. He had an exceptional year as a freshman player and the expectations for his sophomore year were looking good. His father was proud of him and always sat in the same seat for a game. Many times Ted looked up and his father smiled and raise his thumbs. This was all gone now. He had to get on with his life and help his mother as much as he could. There was no use complaining and looking back.

It was different getting on the school bus taking him to his new school. He looked around and saw the many strange faces and took a seat by a window and looked out. He didn't make eye contact with anyone and wondered what his friends were doing back at his former school. It was depressing thinking what he left. His trance broke when a guy's voice from the back of the bus shouted, "Hey! Ugly broad. Were you in an ax fight and you didn't have an ax?"

Ted turned and saw the guy who said it and the boys sitting

around him laughing. The guy shouted again, "I'm talking to you, Nancy Bean Pole. You're so skinny if you drank cherry pop you'd look like a thermometer."

Ted looked across the aisle and saw the girl the remarks were being directed at. She sank down into her seat, squinted her eyes and shook her head. She was slim and not very pretty and wore black horn-rimmed glasses and a bandana. More remarks were yelled. The girl cringed, shivered and a tear ran down her cheek.

Ted looked at the group laughing in the back. He got up and patted the girl on her shoulder than walked to the back of the bus. He pointed his finger in the face of the big mouth. "That girl didn't do anything to you. If you want to pick on someone, try me." The guy kept staring at Ted's clenched fists and didn't say anything. "Well go ahead wise guy. Say something, get up and try me." The group was not laughing now. No one said a word. Ted continued to glare at them, then walked backwards to his seat never taking his eyes off them. He didn't say anything to the girl nor did she say anything to him.

The next morning he got on the bus again. The girl didn't look up at him. She had her hands in her lap and waved with a couple of fingers. Ted touched her shoulder, looked to the back of the bus where big Mouth and his friends were. No one said anything. Every day after that when Ted got on the bus the girl never looked up at him. She kept her hands in her lap and waved in her usual manner with two fingers.

Weeks passed and the only attention Ted got was from the football coach. One day the coach said, "I bet your old team misses you. We feel fortunate having you on our team."

Ted nodded, "I feel bad about leaving my old team and all my friends but if I try hard enough I hope I'll be able to play well here."

"Don't worry about that. You already proved yourself. In fact, you'll be starting as our quarterback next week against Harbor High."

Ted felt out of place when he walked the halls of the

school. The students never said hi.

They had the latest style clothes on. His clothes were clean but were old and a little faded. It was lonely being ignored. He never mentioned this to his mother, she had enough problems.

Friday night the bus transporting the football team parked next to a brightly lit stadium. The team rushed onto the field and the people on the right side of the stadium stood up and cheered. The band exploded with the school fight song. Butterflies were swarming in Ted's stomach, adrenaline was pumping through his veins like lava erupting in a volcano. It felt like his feet weren't touching the ground. It was unreal just like the games back at his old school.

After warm-ups the teams lined up for the start of the game. Ted was on the receiving team and was the deep man. The opposing team kicked the ball and it came to him. He ran up the right side of the field then reversed direction and all at once he was in the open and went into the end zone scoring a touchdown. The man on the P A system yelled. "What a run, a seventy-five yard touchdown by number twenty-six Ted Curtis." The game continued and when it was over Ted scored another touchdown and passed for one. The next day his picture was on the front page of the sports section. Ted saw it and wished his father could be with him.

When Ted came to school Monday everything changed. As he walked down the halls students came up and introduced themselves, mostly girls. He smiled and nodded his head at them. A few of the good-looking ones asked if had a girlfriend. He didn't know what to say. His blood pressure shot up. It was unreal.

Things was perfect for him now. Even though he didn't have the best clothes it didn't matter. He was more then accepted. It was nice going to school. As the football season continued Ted became more popular. Everything was going great until he got a phone call from a girl. At first he didn't recognize who it was, then she said, "You have been so nice to me Ted. Those boys don't call me names anymore."

"That's all right, I'm glad I could help you."

Ted, it was nice of you to ask me to the prom. I never went out with a boy. My mother bought me a new dress and I'm going to get a permanent. Thank you, Ted. You could have asked any girl in school and they would of loved going with you."

Ted was lost for words. He stuttered and mumbled a couple of times then said, "Can I call you back?" His mother sensed something wrong when she saw him just looking at the phone and not saying anything.

"What's the matter, Ted?"

"Nothing, Mom. I got to work something out and I don't know how."

His mother questioned him until he finally said. "Mom, someone called a girl and said it was me. He asked her to go to the prom. She just called and told me she got a new dress and is getting all fixed up for the dance. It was a dirty trick. The girl is nice but she's really homely."

"Well, Ted you can make that young lady very happy if you take her. It will break her heart if you tell her it was a joke."

"I know, Mom. I don't want to hurt her. Guys at school make fun of her and I feel sorry for her."

"Well, you'd be a real man if you take her. I'm sure you'll have a good time."

Two weeks later he went to Nancy's home where he met her parents. Then the couple took a cab to the dance. As soon as they walked in Ted felt every pair of eyes in the place looking at them. Nancy was all smiles. They sat at a table with other football players and their dates. Ted went to get some refreshments and some of the girls came up to him and said. "Ted, I would of been your date if you needed one." He ignored them and went back to his table. He talked with Nancy and she was good company. She was smart and friendly.

Everything was going fine until he left to go to the restroom. The guy with the big mouth came up and said. "I see you took that ugly dog. You wanted to make sure you got some sure stuff."

Ted didn't hesitate. One punch to the big mouth's jaw sent him to the floor. Ted was about to hit him again but one of the coaches grabbed his arm. "No more, Ted. I didn't see who pushed you into that guy. Go back to your table, I'll handle this."

When he got back, Nancy asked, "What happened, Ted? Was you in a fight? Was it the guy who called me those names on the bus?"

"Oh no, there was no fight. Somebody lost his balance and bumped into me. I bumped into him. That's all. No big deal."

Nancy and Ted danced and had fun talking to other players and their dates. Afterwards he took her home. As they walked to the front porch She grabbed both his hands and looked up into his eyes. "Thank you for a wonderful evening. It was the best thing that ever happened to me. I'll remember it for the rest of my life."

He turned. She wrapped her arms around his neck and kissed him. He was spellbound. "It was a nice night, I'll, I'll, I'll see you on the bus." He jumped off the porch shaking and ran home.

****

Six years later Ted was at a nightclub with a bunch of his friends, when a beautiful woman walked up to him. "Do you remember me, Ted?"

Ted's friends blurted out, "Wow, I'd like to remember a dish like that. You're a lucky guy, Ted."

Ted was confused. He could only stare at her. "I'm sorry I don't remember."

"I'm Nancy."

"Nancy?"

"Nancy from the school bus. You took me to the prom when we were in high school. I'll never forget that night."

"Boy, Nancy, You're a beautiful lady."

"Don't ask me what happened but it happened. I've changed and I'm happy."

"And I'll bet you're one happy popular woman."

They talked and reminisced of their school days. After they danced to a few songs they left the club and went to her apartment. This time it wasn't a short kiss and run.

CHAPTER 57
BAD BREATH

It seems that kids in poor neighborhoods quickly pick up nicknames. My old neighborhood was no exception. Some of those names I can't repeat. I would like to introduce you to one of those guys who got the handle, Bad Breath. It was in the early fifties and Bad Breath was a funny character who looked like John Baluschi. He had a stocky-build and was very strong. His body was not the only thing that was strong. His breath was stronger. When he spoke to people they would close one eye and turn away. He used to carry garlic bulbs in his pocket and eat them like peanuts. He was poor like the rest of us and his clothes showed it.

He entertained himself by fighting. He was not a racist but found out early that if he called someone a name about their race or ethnic background it almost always guaranteed a fight. This type of behavior caused Bad Breath to be arrested may times and acquire a long police record.

One day Bad Breath disappeared from the neighborhood. It was like he fell off the earth. Guys asked each other about him, but no one knew what happened.

****

Twenty-five years later I was a detective on the police department and the desk sergeant called over the intercom. He said that an attorney and another guy were on their way back to see me. I watched the hallway and there appeared Bad Breath and one of the most successful lawyers in town. Bad Breath hadn't changed much. His clothing was different. He was wearing an expensive suit and had a fresh haircut. He walked up to my desk and threw out his hand. We shook and he patted my back. "Man, it's good seeing you again. Bob." He turned to the attorney and said. "Me and this guy go back a long way. We grew up in the same neighborhood and were the best of friends. We played a lot of sports together. Them were the days, weren't they, Bob?"

I almost called him Bad Breath but caught myself. "Yeah Mervin, they sure were. We had a lot of good times. What brings you here?"

"Well, I've got a problem that has been haunting me for a long time and I want to get it off my chest and make things right."

The attorney quickly threw up his arms. "Don't say anymore, I'll handle this part."

Bad Breath squinted and pointed at his attorney. "I'll tell you when to talk."

It got quiet. I shrugged my shoulders, "I'll try to help if I can. Let's hear it."

"I skipped town a long time ago. I'll tell you right from the start what happened. There were some arrest warrants out for me and the cops were getting close to catching me. I had to get out of town but I didn't have any money. I decided to rob somebody and use the money to buy a bus ticket. It was dark and I found a big board in an alley. I picked it up and hid behind a tree. I saw this guy walking on the sidewalk. I snuck up behind him and tried to whack him in the head. The guy was big and I hit him in the shoulder. I underestimated him. He took the board away from me and pounded hell out of me with it. I limped downtown to the bus station and I bumped into some guy in the parking lot. He got mad and we fought. He almost punched me to death. I was hurt bad and crawled onto an empty bus and laid on a seat in the back. I passed out and when I awoke the bus was moving. There were people on it.

I stayed on the bus for a couple of days and noticed the bus driver looking at me in his rearview mirror. I thought he was going to call the cops, so when the bus stopped for a red light, I opened the window and jumped out. I ran for a couple of blocks and saw a large group of people standing in front of an old building. I walked up to some guys and I asked them why all those people were standing in front of that old barn. Man, those guys went crazy. One of them shouted, "You must be one of those stupid Yankees. 'That's the Alamo. You Jerk." They jumped me and beat me to a pulp. I crawled to a curb and sat down and rubbed my wounds. A brand new expensive car stopped. A guy got out and asked if he could help me.

I said, "Yeah, get me the hell out of here."

The guy must of felt sorry for me. He put me up and taught me his business fixing up old cars and selling them. I learned real well and I got my own business, and it grew and grew. I made a lot of money. Now I want to use that money to clear up the things I did wrong here."

I advised him I would have to go to the record bureau and look up the old reports concerning him and get back with him. Before he left, he pointed out the window. "That's my car, Bob." It was a Rolls Royce. It took me two days to locate the reports and warrants concerning Bad Breath. Most of them the Statue of Limitations had run out.

I called the victims and some had passed away. Others said they were not interested anymore and didn't want to prosecute. The guy who hit Bad Breath with the board said. "The only reason he made out a police report was he felt he might have killed the guy who hit him." Only one person wanted to reopen his case.

I called Bad Breath and explained the matter. An hour passed. The victim called and said he was contacted by Bad Breath's attorney and the matter was settled. I asked, "What about the medical bills?" The victim said the attorney was very generous.

Bad Breath was grateful everything was cleared up. We drove through the old neighborhood. We laughed as we reminisced about things we did when we were young.

Before he left I took a bulb of garlic out of my pocket and dangled it in front of his nose. He in turn took my wallet out of his pocket and dangled it. The damn fool had pickpocketed me.

CHAPTER 58
REPOSSESSION

Carl Mchaffie pulled the letter from the mailbox and read the upper left corner of the envelope. *Lazer Finance Company.* Right away he knew he had a problem. He opened the envelope and unfolded the letter. His eyes focused on the bold paragraph, **Pay past due payments or your car will be repossessed after ten days of this dated letter.**

Carl slapped the letter on the palm of his hand. *Man, what the hell am I going to do. I don't have any money and I sure as hell don't want to lose what I got invested in that car.* He tried to sell it but there were no takers. He then remembered the old quarry where he use to swim. It was deep and if he drove it in there, no one would ever find it and the insurance company would pay for his car.

Driving to the quarry, he thought how he'd sink the car. The walls surrounding the quarry were high and it was encircled by tall trees. There was only one road leading to it. *I'll park the car about fifteen feet from the edge and leave it running. I'll get out and put it into drive and watch it go over the edge. It'll drop into the water, sink and no one will ever see it again. I'll call the insurance company and say, someone stole my car.*

When he got to the unpaved road leading back to the quarry, he turned onto it and drove about twenty feet and was met by a steel fence blocking the road. In the middle of the fence was a sign that read. **No Trespassing, Violators Will Be Prosecuted.** He punched the steering wheel and yelled, "Damn."

For the next two days all his thoughts were how to salvage his money invested in that car. All at once he remembered the county road with the railroad crossing. There were no warning signs at this crossing and the trains traveled at a high rate of speed. If one of those fast trains plowed into his car it would demolish it and the railroad would pay for it. He had to find a way to have the car moving when the train hits it. If it was parked on the tracks the engineer might see it and slam on the brakes. At first he thought he'd drive it in front of the speeding train and would protect himself from the impact by rolling up in a mattress. Then he thought, what would he tell the rescue people when they saw him inside the demolished car rolled up in a mattress.

He liked the idea of the train destroying his car but he had to find a way for the car to be moving when the train hit it. He pondered the thought until he saw a kid roller-skating. He shouted. "That's it."

He bought a pair of roller-skates and a broom then drove to the isolated train crossing. He put the skates on and had the broom ready on the front seat. After two hours he saw the train in the distance. Everything was perfect. There was no one around. The train was about a hundred yards from the crossing. The motor of the car was running. Carl was on the outside reaching through the front window. He pushed the gas pedal down with the broom stick. The car lurched toward the track and Carl steered through the window. He thought, *Everything is going perfect. All I got to do is steer the car to the tracks and then I'll roll away from it on the skates right before the train hits it.* Everything was going as planned until Carl's one skate dropped into a pot hole. The skate stopped abruptly and Carl's knee buckled. Inadvertently his hands pulled down on the steering wheel causing the car to make a sharp left turn into a cornfield. The speeding train passed with its horn blasting. The engineer was hanging out the window shaking his fist. Carl picked himself up and pulled the corn leaves off. His car was still running.

He quickly took off the skates and ran to his car and put it in reverse and backed out onto the road. *Got to get out of here before the farmer comes and makes me pay for the corn. The engineer on that train probably has a phone and is calling the cops.*

Being desperate Carl was ready to give up and let them repossess his car. It was two o'clock in the morning and he was taking a last drive. He abruptly stopped the car and watched a drunk stagger out of a tavern. The guy bounced off the building a coupe times then managed to straighten up and get to his car. He fumbled in his pockets until he found his car keys, then pushed the key into the side door numerous times until he found the keyhole. After some swearing he managed to open the door. Finally opening the door he fell into a white Ford. His head wobbled a few times but somehow managed to start the car. Carl quickly did a U-turn and parked. He watched the white Ford come out of the tavern parking lot and make a right turn onto Superior Street. Carl quickly drove to Summit Street that ran parallel to Superior Street and made a right turn.

While driving, Carl thought of all the streets that crossed Superior Street that had traffic lights. The first one was Bush Street. He turned right onto Bush and waited. In a short time he saw the headlights of the white Ford coming. The drunk had the green light and was approaching the intersection. Carl had the red light but drove in front of the drunk and put on the brakes. He shut his eyes, cringed and waited for the impact. A loud screeching of tires but no collision. Carl slowly opened his eyes and saw the drunk's car inches away from his car. The drunk's head wobbled and slurred something.

Carl shouted, "Damn," then spun his tires and drove back to Summit Street and turned onto Ontario Street and waited for the drunk. The white Ford again had the green light. Carl ran the red light and stopped directly in the path of the other car. The drunk swerved his car and went over the curb onto the sidewalk and bounced back into the street. Carl punched the steering wheel again, "Damn."

Carl was discouraged but he kept thinking of the

repossession company taking his car and losing his money. He thought, *Got to do something different. I'll get in front of him and slam on the brakes and he'll rear end me.* Carl passed the white Ford and as planned he jammed the brakes on. He sunk in his seat, closed his eyes and waited for the impact. The screech of tires and the white Ford barely touched his back bumper. Carl shouted, "Damn, you gotta do better then that. I need a total on this car or the insurance company will just fix the damage. He got in front of the drunk a couple more times and jammed his breaks but the drunk managed to stop in time.

Carl shook his head. *Got to go back to the original plan. It has to be a broadside.* He drove to the next intersection with a traffic light and waited. This time the drunk stopped because he was facing a red light. Carl waited until the light turned green for the drunk. The white Ford started into the intersection. Carl drove in front of it and stopped. The white Ford's tires screeched as it came to a stop inches from Carl's car. The door flew open on the white Ford and the drunk came out. He threw his keys in the air and slurred. "Screw this, I'm getting a cab."

Two officers were in a parking lot with the headlights out on their car. They were making out reports by the light of their clip boards. They both looked up when they heard the squealing tires. They saw the whole thing and ran to the cars. They asked Carl what he was doing. Carl shrugged and his hands were palms up. He was so discouraged he told the whole account of why he did it.

The driver of the white Ford staggered to the officers. His head wobbled a coupled times until he got the officers in focus. He blurted out, "I'm drunk and I almost caused twenty accidents. I give up."

Printed in the United States
76780LV00002B/135

9 781432 701864